The Affair
at
Lime Hill

I0733697

Jeremy
Akerman

© 2023 Jeremy Akerman

All rights reserved. No part of this book may be reproduced or transmitted in any form or by any means, electronic or mechanical, including photocopying, or by any information storage or retrieval system, without permission in writing from the publisher.

Cover image: "The Glory of Fall" by the author
Cover design: Rebekah Wetmore
Interior images by the author

Editor: Andrew Wetmore

ISBN: 978-1-990187-74-2
First edition March, 2023

2475 Perotte Road
Annapolis County, NS
B0S 1A0

moosehousepress.com
info@moosehousepress.com

We live and work in Mi'kma'ki, the ancestral and unceded territory of the Mi'kmaw People. This territory is covered by the "Treaties of Peace and Friendship" which Mi'kmaw and Wolastoqiyik (Maliseet) People first signed with the British Crown in 1725. The treaties did not deal with surrender of lands and resources but in fact recognized Mi'kmaq and Wolastoqiyik (Maliseet) title and established the rules for what was to be an ongoing relationship between nations. We are all Treaty people.

Also by Jeremy Akerman

and available from Moose House Publications

Memoir
Outsider

Politics
What Have You Done for Me Lately? - revised edition

Fiction
Black Around the Eyes – revised edition
The Premier's Daughter
Finding Doctor Dee (coming in 2023)

Dedicated to my beloved Caroll Anne

and in memory of
Gareth Edward Akerman 1974-2008
Michael John Akerman 1938-2021

This is a work of fiction. The author has created the characters, conversations, interactions, and events, and any resemblance of any character to any real person is coincidental.

The Affair at Lime Hill

West Bay from Marble Mountain

Jeremy Akerman

1: Arm of Gold

It was a perfect fall day. Most of the leaves were becoming a delicate lemon yellow, positively gleaming in the sunlight, and gently swaying in the soft breeze. Here and there the occasional leaf shone out in orange amid the rich, deep green of the spruce which climbed the steep sides on either side of the water. Lower down, near the shore, some patches of grass were a pale gold while others had already become ochre.

Dotted about the shore, sheep lazily grazed, apparently oblivious of their idyllic surroundings; but the cows were sensibly lying under the shade of the large maples, their slightly swishing tails the only apparent signs of life. High above, gulls, terns and crows competed in spectacular feats of aerobatics, sometimes appearing to bounce off the light fluffy clouds.

Cape Breton Island's Bras D'Or Lakes stretched as far as the eye could see until they disappeared, merging into the pale azure horizon. The first white men to see this expanse of water are said to have been French explorers who came here in the 1580s. Supposedly, they saw the lakes reflecting the sun and called them *Bras d'or*, or "Arm of gold".

The sun, now starting to sink in the sky, cast a ribbon of gold across the surface of the sparkling blue water, picking out on the north shore dozens of miniature wharves, fields, farms, and houses.

Far in the distance, one house was barely distinguishable from a dozen others scattered along the shore of Lime Hill by a faint, flashing blue light. This emanated from the roof of an ambulance which was parked in the yard of an old farm, about a kilometre from the water's edge. A short dirt driveway connected the farm and its weathered outbuildings with a small secondary road. This was the Old Gillis Place, where some seven generations of that clan had lived and worked.

The sound of slamming doors and loud sobbing came from within the darkened recesses of the residence.

2: A call from home

Toronto was unbearable. The heat was stifling, and the sun beat down on baked, dusty streets, its blinding light reflecting from cars, windows, buses and trucks. The heavy, noisy traffic belched stinky exhaust fumes into an atmosphere which was barely moving. The shimmering sidewalks were thick with sweating pedestrians, their clothing in disarray as they struggled to their destinations.

The city desperately needed a good, cleansing downpour, but weather forecasts were not obliging and were condemning the citizens to several more weeks of suffering.

Detective Sergeant Roberta Gillis and her sidekick, Gordon Wadden, were stuck in a traffic jam. In the last ten minutes they had moved no more than half a kilometre and, since the congestion was equally bad in both directions, there was nothing they could accomplish by switching on their flasher. Although the air conditioner was on full blast, the heat in the police cruiser was overwhelming, sweat was trickling down Roberta's neck, and both she and Gordon were starting to smell.

Roberta was a slim, attractive, dark-haired woman about forty, wearing a light cotton dress, while Gordon was an overweight, balding man in his fifties whose heavy, noisy breathing was getting on her nerves. She and Gordon had been partners for almost three years, during which time she had been exasperated by his habits and grateful for his courage and loyalty in equal measure. He could be a real pain in the rear end, but was magnificent in emergencies. He might look like a boozer who had gone to seed, she thought, but he's like a Tasmanian devil when the chips are down.

To add to their present discomfort, in the back of the cruiser they had in handcuffs Harvey, a repeat offender whose habits and personal hygiene left much to be desired. He was dirty, unkempt and unshaven, with breath redolent of some unspeakable variety of alcohol.

"If youse had asked me," he slurred, "I could have showed youse a short cut to the police station."

"Shut your mouth," snapped Gordon, "You're in enough trouble already!"

"Juss tryin' to be helpful," said Harvey.

Roberta mopped the back of her neck with a

handkerchief. When she looked at it, it was soaking wet.

Glancing out of the car window she noticed a large billboard advertising an airline. It depicted two smiling—and obviously cool—people on a pink beach with palm trees leaning toward a turquoise sea. HAVE AN ADVENTURE—GET AWAY FROM IT ALL was the caption.

"What a great idea," she said, "I sure wish I was there now. I could use some R and R. Any sign of movement up ahead, Gordon?"

"Not yet. Probably some damn truck overturned, I shouldn't wonder."

"It's not toxic waste, is it?" piped up Harvey from the back.

"What the hell you talking about?" Gordon said, irritated. "I thought I told you to keep quiet."

"Youse said a truck overturned. Maybe it spilled toxic waste."

"Shut your mouth. Or I'll ram toxic waste down your throat."

They sat there breathing heavily, the sweat now pouring down their faces, the odour from Harvey becoming sickening. Gordon stuck his arm out of the window and starting pounding his fist against the door.

"Say, have you seen that show?" Harvey asked,

pointing to another billboard advertising a performance of *Dr. Jekyll and Mr Hyde.* "That show. You seen it?"

"Jesus Christ! If you don't shut up...."

Roberta put a hand on Gordon's arm to restrain him.

"Which was the bad guy? Jekyll or Hyde?" Harvey persisted.

"Hyde," said Roberta.

Gordon buried his face in his hands.

"Sounds like it should be the other way round," said Harvey.

"Yes, I always thought that too." said Roberta with a heavy sigh.

"Jekyll is a meaner soundin' name than Hyde, ain't it?"

"If you don't shut your goddamned mouth," Gordon exploded, "there's going to be some police brutality around here!"

Harvey cowered back into the seat. Roberta put her head back and closed her eyes. All she could hear now was the cacophony of car horns blowing.

~

It was over an hour later when they got to the station. They dragged a kicking and shouting Harvey to the duty sergeant, booked him, saw him delivered to the cells, then clambered upstairs to the squad room.

It was a clamorous, hot, sweltering bedlam of crowded desks, computers and cabinets with ineffectual fans whose only accomplishment seemed to be blowing papers into disorganized heaps. Officers and clerks were scurrying around, a choir of phones were ringing in unison and people were shouting at each other, angrily demanding attention. A small terrier tied to the leg of a desk was yapping incessantly. In one corner a little old lady sat alone, sobbing uncontrollably.

As Roberta entered she saw a colleague, Jenny, waving to her from the other end of the room, so, exchanging small talk as she went, she threaded her way through the throng to her.

"What's up, Jenny?"

"Your brother wants you to call him right away."

"My brother, Rod? He called here?"

"Yeah."

"That's weird. What did he want?"

"Don't know. He didn't say. Just said it was urgent. That was a couple of hours ago."

"Okay, thanks, Jenny."

Roberta withdrew into her "office", which was basically a three-sided cubicle formed by movable partitions and furniture. Standing at her desk, she rummaged through her bag for her address book. It had, she was ashamed to admit, been so long since she had called Rod and Shirley, his wife, that she had forgotten the number.

She hung her bag on the back of a large swivel chair, sat down and pulled the phone towards her. There was no answer for several seconds, then Rod came on the line.

"Hello."

"Hey Rod. It's me. I only just got your message. What's going on?"

"It's Shirley, Bobby. She's dead."

"Dead?"

"She died about four hours ago."

"What? Oh my God. Oh Rod I'm so very sorry. What happened?"

"They don't know for sure yet." Rod's voice sounded weak. "The doctor thinks she must have had some kind of freak aneurysm. He tried to explain it, I but I couldn't really understand. He says they'll know for sure later."

"Oh Roddy, you poor thing. How are the kids taking it?"

"Not too well, Angie is in a terrible state."

"Poor little mite. Give her my love. What about Ma?"

"She's out of it. With that Alzheimer's she has no

idea what's going on."

"Is there anything I can do?"

"Yes, by Jesus, there is." Rod raised his voice. "You can get back here right away and look after the kids and the old woman. I've got to work to pay the bills. I'm working down at the strait now and they won't hold my job for me if I take time off."

"I don't see how I could, Rod. My case load is sky high. I just can't"

"Bobby, just fucking do it, Bobby. For Christ's sake!"

The line went dead. Rod had other things to attend to, and he was in no mood to argue.

~

Inspector Cyril Caduggan had a proper office with walls, a door, and even a window which backed on a quadrangle of weeds surrounded by pipes and wires. Today, the sun streamed through, making bright patterns on the old ragged carpet.

Caduggan was a very large, burly man in his late forties, a terse, to-the-point, man who did not suffer fools gladly, but who possessed reserves of kindness for his favourite employees. Roberta preened herself because she was sure that she was one of the chosen.

After he heard about the circumstances of Shirley's death, Caduggan did not beat about the bush. "I know what you want me to say."

"Oh? What do I want you to say?"

"You want me to say that I can't spare you, that we can't get by without you. That it's administratively impossible."

"Do I?" Roberta asked, hoping that he would say exactly that.

"Yes, you know you do. Admit it."

"Well, my caseload is enormous, so it is administratively impossible."

"I won't bullshit you, Roberta, that's not my style. You're good and you'll be missed. But you're not indispensable. It can be fixed."

Roberta's heart sank. She felt wounded by his comments. Cyril knew how to hurt.

"Look, you've got vacation time owed you and compassionate leave is in the collective agreement. A month is no problem at all. Beyond that, I would have to work something out with City Hall."

Roberta, angry with herself and with Caduggan, stared at him resentfully.

"You've got responsibilities to your family. Go discharge them with a willing heart, for God's sake. Your job will still be here."

She felt as she had when a teacher had castigated her for some classroom misdemeanour. But as uncomfortable as it felt, she knew he was right. She hated to leave her work and utterly dreaded the difficult, but humdrum, existence she would endure on the farm. Washing, cooking, cleaning, getting children off to school, and dealing with a woman who no longer recognized her filled her with profound gloom. But she knew she had to do it.

~

Later that evening, Rod Gillis was standing in the kitchen, aimlessly looking out of the window at the turning leaves and the glistening water beyond. Some crows were arguing with a heron, chasing it as if it had violated their territory. Further out, a small fishing boat from the We'koqma'q reserve was slowly making its way home.

Rod was a healthy, fit man in his mid-forties, used to manual labour and outdoor work of all kinds. As he always did, he wore work pants and a plaid flannel shirt. The last time he had put on a suit or worn a tie was when his father, Robert, had died many years before.

Behind him, through the open door to the living room, his children sprawled about in front of the television. Bonnie, the oldest at fifteen, red faced with tears, was sitting on the chesterfield, the sobbing head of eight-year-old Angie buried in her lap. On the floor, in front of the television sat Brad, thirteen, vacantly staring ahead. When the phone rang, none of them reacted, because they expected it would be yet another neighbour offering commiserations. On hearing their father say Roberta's name the two girls ran into the kitchen where they stood expectantly, watching him speak.

"Rod, I've got a month, maybe a bit more in a pinch."

"That's great Bobby. Thanks a million." Rod rubbed his eyes with the back of his hand.

"It means I have to take a day or two here to tie up loose ends. When's the funeral?"

"Thursday." Rod put his arm around Angie, who was now hanging off the arm of his chair.

"I'll have to miss it. You understand?"

"Yeah. I'll explain it to the kids."

"I'll be there around early evening on Sunday if everything goes according to plan. Okay?"

"Sure. See you then, Sis."

They hung up simultaneously.

Bonnie sat down in the opposite chair. "Is she coming?"

"Yes, your Aunty Bob says she will be here on Sunday."

"That'll be good," Bonnie pronounced firmly.

"Angie, you're too little to remember Aunty Bob."

"Am not. I love Aunty Bob," Angie said in a tiny, far-away voice.

"We all do, honey," Rod said.

3: Along the Saint Lawrence

Roberta was fortunate in getting away from the city at the time she had planned. She was even more fortunate that the traffic was not as bad as she feared, although the 401 was slow for some reason between Kingston and Cornwall, and again in the approaches to Montreal. She remembered having once driven the entire distance from Toronto to Cape Breton non-stop, and certainly had no intention of repeating the ordeal. Several times, she recalled, she had to slap her own face to try to stay awake.

She had Googled to see where the halfway point was between Toronto and Cape Breton, and discovered it was at Saint Jean Port Joli on the shores of the St. Lawrence. Then she had searched overnight accommodation in the area and had settled upon a motel called L'Auberge Marie, which she had called to reserve a room.

It was fairly plain sailing along the TransCanada Highway and she kept to a steady 100 kph, but she counted twenty-eight enormous trucks which came thundering past her, heading for unknown destinations.

Turning off the highway, she drove through Saint Jean Port Joli and along the 123 until she reached her motel. It was spectacularly located, being only metres from the river's edge with an amazing view of Ilot à Chatigny, the larger L'isle aux Coudres, and the pretty north-shore townships of Baie St Paul and Petite Rivière St François. What fabulous names they all have, she thought, each of them conjuring up cliché visions of *habitants* wearing nightcaps, carting wood and ice fishing.

As she was checking in, Roberta asked about dinner arrangements, and learned they could not provide meals because the kitchen was undergoing repairs. The proprietor told her that if she had her own supplies, she could use the barbecue grill at the rear of the motel. Since she had no supplies and did not want to drive back into town to get some, Roberta resigned herself to going to bed without any supper.

As she turned away from the desk, an elderly couple who had been looking at maps in the lobby came up to her.

"Hello," said the man, "I'm Fred Broussard. This is my wife, Louise. We couldn't help overhearing your conversation with the owner. We've got plenty of food. You're welcome to join us at the barbecue."

"You're very kind, but I couldn't possibly intrude."

"You wouldn't be intruding," said Louise putting a kindly hand on her arm. "Fred and I would be glad of the company."

"Well, if you're absolutely sure. I'm starving," said Roberta.

"Let's go round back and fire her up," said Fred.

At the barbecue, as the Broussards laid out their supplies on an old picnic table, Roberta discovered that they had not been exaggerating when they said had plenty. Not only did they have steaks and dessert, but wine, too.

"We're from the United States," said Louise, "from Louisiana. Lafayette, Louisiana."

"You're a long way from home," Roberta observed. "What are you doing way up here?"

"Searching for our roots," Fred said. "We heading down to Nova Scotia. Do you know it?"

"Actually I'm going there myself. I was born there."

"Really? Is that so? Well, you'll know all about the Acadians."

"A fair amount," said Roberta. "I guess you must be Acadians yourselves."

"Yes, sir. Indeed we are. My ancestor was Jean-

François Broussard, who came to Port Royal in 1671. One of his descendants came down to Attakapas County, Louisiana in the 1760s and set up shop at Côté Gelée, which is right near the present town of Broussard, in Lafayette parish."

"So we're going down to see where the first Broussard landed," added Louise.

"That's marvelous," said Roberta, "you must tell me more about your family."

"Sure," said Fred, "but first let's eat. You like filet mignon?"

"Love it. Rare if possible."

"The only way to have it!" declared Fred.

Having devoured the very fine filet mignon which Fred cooked for her, and consumed several glasses of the excellent bottle of Clos St. Denis 2016, Roberta thanked her hosts and withdrew to her room. The room was decent and the bed was firm. The lights were out before ten.

The next day she was up early. It was a splendid day with high skies and few clouds. A large ship was nosing its way up the river toward Quebec and a flock of geese loudly honked their way in the opposite direction. Since she could hardly expect the Broussards to cook for her again this morning, she planned to head out immediately and get some breakfast on the road.

When she was younger, Roberta had made a name for herself as a singer and performer. She only played in Cape Breton but was generally considered to be good. As she drove along the Saint Lawrence, Roberta thought of those days, threw back her head and warbled like a bird:

> *The water is wide, I cannot get over*
> *Neither have I wings to fly*
> *Give me a boat that can carry two*
> *And both shall row, my love and I*
>
> *I leaned my back against an oak*
> *Thinking it was a trusty tree*
> *But first it bent and then it broke*
> *So did my love prove false to me*
>
> *Oh love be handsome and love be kind*
> *Gay as a jewel when first it is new*
> *But love grows old and waxes cold*
> *And fades away like the morning dew*
>
> *When cockle shells turn silver bells*
> *Then will my love come back to me*
> *When roses bloom in winter's gloom*
> *Then will my love return to me*

There was even less traffic now, and as she drove she encountered more magical names on the passing road signs. She particularly liked Kamouraska, Nôtre-Dame-du-Portage, and Saint-Honoré-de-Te-mis-couta. Her rudimentary knowledge of French caused her to wonder about the origins of some of the place names. What was the joke which gave its name to Village de La Blague? Was there still a bottle factory in Saint Denis de la Bouteillière? Her favourite was Saint Louis du Ha! Ha!

She recalled that, following the first time she had passed this way, she had looked it up and found that it was the only place in the world with two exclamation points in its name, and was actually in the *Guinness Book of Records*.

She would have liked to make a detour to see St. Louis du Ha! Ha!, but she knew she didn't have time to make a detour if she wanted to reach her destination before nightfall.

The drive through eastern Quebec and then New Brunswick was tiring, and she was developing an ache between her shoulder blades, but the glints of gold in the trees and the occasional glimpses of lakes and rivers relieved the monotony.

When she finally saw the "Welcome to Nova Scotia" sign at Aulac, her spirits momentarily lifted, but by the time she had crossed the Canso Causeway, dragged herself through Port Hawkesbury and got to Cleveland she was cranky and exhausted. There, she turned off on to the secondary road to West Bay and, as the light was fading, headed up the magical slope to Lime Hill, the site of her childhood and the place of many memories, both good and bad.

Home at last.

4: Home

The old Gillis place was set in a lovely spot on a hill of birches, overlooking the Bras D'Or Lakes. The last of the day's sun, now in sharp decline, shafted through the yellowing leaves, dappling the roadway with dancing patterns.

Even though Roberta hadn't been home for two years, she thought she couldn't miss the house and the barn and the small garden in front, but she was wrong and twice she almost turned into the wrong yards.

She felt a few pangs as she passed Dan MacIsaac's smartly-painted cabin, surrounded by a huge lawn at the water's edge. She and Dan had history. Not as much as Dan would have liked, but they had known and respected each other ever since Roberta was a teenager.

Dan was why she joined the police, and he had been the one to whom she had turned whenever she needed advice. He was recently retired from the

RCMP, she had heard, having taken a reduced pension five years early. She would definitely be making an early call on Dan, she told herself, although she was somewhat apprehensive about his feelings towards her and wondered how much he had changed.

When she was younger, she had been less sensitive to the feelings of others, and especially to men whom she knew were attracted to her. She had thought that a little mild flirting did no harm, but in Dan's case it had created something of a problem which, she conceded, she had done little to solve.

In any event, she thought, Dan *was* a big boy and their long term friendship was not likely to be impaired.

Then suddenly there it was!

Rod and Angie were sitting on the top of the front steps reading one of her books, while Brad was slouched on the bottom step idly poking a flower bed with a stick. Bonnie was slowly dribbling a soccer ball up ahead. She looked up, saw the car and shouted to the others.

"She's here! I think this is her!" she cried, running toward the house.

Roberta gave a few toots on the horn and slowly pulled into the driveway. Rod rose and walked forward, Angie pushing ahead of him.

When she got out of the car, Rod and the girls milled around her. Picking up Angie and balancing her on one hip, Roberta exchanged hugs and kisses with Rod and Bonnie.

Noticing Brad still sitting on the bottom step, she put Angie down and went up to him. "Is this Brad? It can't be, he's so big. Look at the size of him. How are you, buddy?"

"How do you think?" Brad responded without looking at her.

"I know, honey," she said, sitting beside him. "I'm awful sorry."

"Yeah." He was surly and out of sorts.

Roberta rose and cast a glance at Rod who met her gaze with a shrug. He motioned her into the house and, dragging her luggage, they all traipsed in.

"We waited supper for you," said Rod as he slung Roberta's cases into the hall closet. "I've got stew ready to go, so you can sort your stuff out later."

"You are an angel," said Roberta. "I'm absolutely starving."

"Can I sit by you, Aunty Bob?" asked Angie rather plaintively.

"Of course you can, sweetheart. Come and show me where."

They all seemed to have enormous appetites. Rod, Brad and Bonnie ate heartily and Roberta wolfed hers down. The rich, aromatic, dark brown stew, and chunks of home-made bread left by a kindly neighbour went down a treat.

When they had finished eating, Brad and Bonnie charged into the other room and switched on the television. Angie climbed up into Roberta's lap.

"Will you put me to bed tonight, Aunty Bob?"

"Certainly I will, my darling, but you run along and watch TV now. Daddy and I have some things we need to talk over."

Reluctantly, the child disentangled herself, slid to the floor and slowly left them.

"How was the funeral?"

"Desperate," replied Rod. "The kids were a mess, and I wasn't much better."

"Where'd you have it, St. Joseph's?"

"Yeah. I swear Father MacIntyre forgot who he was talking about during the eulogy."

"Is he still around? He must be a hundred."

"Pretty near, I guess. And he had to read the whole service off cards. You'd think he'd know it by heart, he's done it so many times."

They looked at each other in silence for a few minutes, then Rod said, "Thanks for doing this."

"It's okay, but don't forget it's only for a month, for sure."

"Well, do what you can."

"Let's wait and see," said Roberta.

Roberta noticed that Rod was staring at her and grinning broadly. "What?"

"Nothing."

"Come on, what is it?"

"The way you're talking. Ontario talk. Never know you were a Cape Bretoner."

"Well, I've been gone a long time."

"Have you ever! It's been two years since you were last here. Angie was almost a baby."

"That long? I guess you're right. You'll have to bring me up to speed. Give me all the dirt and gossip. Who's misbehaving."

"The MacDonalds, as always," said Rod with a laugh.

"Randy and Lavendar. They still screwing everybody in sight?"

"And each other, I shouldn't wonder."

Roberta hooted and punched Rod's arm. "How's Lolly?"

"She doesn't seem to mind what Randy and Lavvy get up to. I've a mind she was that way herself when she was younger. Maybe still is, for all I know. They do say that the kids are from different fathers."

"I'll go and see them tomorrow," said Roberta. "Is Skit still with them?"

"Yeah, poor bastard. Crazy as ever. And you can hardly understand a word he says."

"Poor old Skit. How about Linus?"

"Oh, he's alright. Still out in his shed. Must be ninety-something now."

"And Danny?" Roberta asked casually, not wanting to imply anything by her tone.

"Danny who?"

"Danny MacIsaac."

"The old Mountie? I guess he's alright. I see him around now and then. I recall you and him were pretty tight one time."

"Yes."

"Something going on there between you two?"

"I'm not sure what you mean," replied Roberta, knowing she was blushing.

"So there *was* something going on!"

"Not in the way you mean, Rod. We were very close friends over a long period of time, that's all."

"Probably just as well. He's got a good fifteen years on you."

Roberta got up and walked to the stove to pour herself a cup of tea, asking herself why she was suddenly annoyed by what Rod had said. "You want one?"

"No, thanks."

When she returned they sat in silence for several minutes. Finally, Rod piped up. "Forgot to tell you. We've got new neighbours."

"Who?"

"John Sedgemoor and his wife. They bought the old Ferguson place about a year ago and fixed it up really nice."

"John Sedgemoor. Why do I know that name?"

"He was the butler in *Hampton Nights*. Remember?"

"The television series? Good God. I do remember him, I used to watch that show religiously. He was a hunk. Really handsome."

"He's a pillar of the community now. Volunteer fireman and everything. Fitted in just like an old shirt. I wish I could say the same for his wife."

"Why? What's wrong with her?"

"You'll find out soon enough. Right contrary, she

is, and puts on airs and graces."

"Well, life is full of surprises. Imagine: John Sedge-moor living here."

There was another awkward silence. Rod looked at her pointedly. "Got to be done. No point in putting it off."

"You're right," she said, knowing exactly what he meant.

"She won't know you from the man in the moon, so you'd better prepare yourself. It's right sad."

"Okay."

The room at the eastern side of the house was at the end of a long, rather dark corridor. Roberta gently tapped at the door, knowing there would be no response, then gingerly entered.

At the large window of the sparsely-furnished room sat a woman in her eighties, gently rocking in an enormous chair. Dressed in a voluminous white gown, she stared vacantly into the now well advanced night.

"Hi Ma," said Roberta softly. "It's me, Roberta."

The old lady continued to rock, giving no sign of interest or recognition.

Roberta crouched down by the side of the chair, touching her mother's and kissing her parched, violet-hued cheek. "I love you, Ma."

The woman carried on rocking, still staring into

the night.

"It's no use, Bobby," said Rod, who had followed his sister upstairs, with Angie in tow. "She has no idea where she is, or who we are."

Roberta raised herself with a sigh as Angie wrapped her arms around her.

"Aunty Bob, will you come and tuck me in?"

"Okay, sweetheart. You get into bed and I'll be right there."

She watched Angie leave, then turned to Rod. "Why have you kept her here, Roddie? I mean, if she's unaware of her surroundings, does it matter where she is?"

"No. I guess not. It just didn't seem right putting her in a home."

"You're a kind man, little brother, that's why I love you so much."

Rod looked at the floor, saying nothing. Their mother continued to rock, in a world of her own, a world without knowledge, without meaning and, Roberta devoutly hoped, a world without fear or pain.

"We're going to have to do it now, aren't we?" she said.

"Yes, I guess so. Will you take care of that…while you're here?"

"I will. Are there any, er, facilities around here?"

"Baddeck for sure and, I think, Port Hawkesbury."

"Okay."

Arm in arm they left the bleak room, softly closing the door behind them. Just before they went, their mother appeared to move her head as if she had seen something outside.

But it was an illusion.

~

Angie's was a small but cozy, pretty room tucked under the rafters. A dormer window opened on to the yard and road. All around was a congregation, a veritable army, of stuffed toys of every description, and on the walls were framed prints of picture book characters.

She was in bed, just her face showing above the brightly coloured coverlet. Roberta sat down and gave her a little kiss.

"Aunty Bob?"

"Yes, sweetheart?"

"Bonnie says Mommy is never going to come back. Is that true?"

"Yes, sweetheart," said Roberta fighting to avoid crying, "I'm afraid it is true. I'm very, very sorry."

Tears welled up in Angie's eyes and rolled down her pink cheeks. She sniffled into the sheet.

"You must be a very brave little girl, Angie. That's what your Mommy would want you to do."

"Are you going to live with us now, Aunty Bob?"

"Yes, honey. For a while. About a month, I think. To look after you."

"Will you stay longer if I want you to?"

"We'll have to see, darling. Now you go to sleep. Nighty-night."

Roberta gave her another kiss, and Angie rolled over and closed her eyes.

As she closed Angie's door and started downstairs, Roberta heard voices coming from Brad's room.

"What's *she* doing here? She's not my mother." Brad sounded angry, defiant.

"Keep your voice down," said Rod. "I need her here, Brad. I can't manage on my own. I need her."

"Well *I* don't need her and I don't want her!"

Roberta tip-toed downstairs and was standing by the kitchen window when Rod came back down. Immediately, he noticed the distressed look on his sister's face.

"I guess you heard what Brad said."

Roberta nodded, stifling a sob.

"I thought I heard you going past the door. What can I say? He just needs time. We all do."

"I guess so."

"You've got the other two eating out of your hand. Two out of three is not bad for starters."

"I'll take it," said Roberta. Then, "I think I'll go out for a bit."

"Now? Where're you going? You must be tired out."

"Actually, I am shattered, but I have to look in on Dan."

"Oh. I see." Rod gave her a knowing and rather unpleasant wink. "Danny Fiddles!"

"Why do you call him that?"

"His grandfather and father were both good fiddle players. The whole family is known as Fiddles."

"Oh yes. I'd forgotten that. Although he doesn't play himself."

"No, I guess he's the exception in that clan."

"I'm off, then."

"How long will you be?"

"Well, I won't be spending the night, if that's what you're thinking. I'll be about an hour."

"I'll wait up for you," said Rod as Roberta slipped on her sweater, "there are a few other things we should settle tonight."

5: Something in the shadows

The moon was temporarily obscured by cloud cover, so the road was inky black. Used to living in the city for so long, Roberta took a few minutes to get used to walking without light, but soon she was acclimatized and got her bearings.

As she left the yard, a light breeze from the lakes gently rustled in the trees overhead and, humming to herself, headed down the long hill to Dan's place.

Suddenly, something—a sound, a movement— made her stop dead, staring into the impenetrable blackness of the roadside. There in the woods was what might have been the shadowy bulk of a person.

"Hello," she called. "Who's there? Is there anyone there?"

Only the breeze and what could have been frogs replied. It was difficult to tell, but the shadow might have changed position slightly.

She stared again, but now there was nothing. Chastising herself for being foolish, she quickly hurried on down the hillside until she came to Dan MacIsaac's property.

Here there was more moonlight because Dan's cabin was close to the edge of the lake at some distance from the trees. It was a large, smart, modern cabin with a wooden deck around three sides. On the deck was a big barbecue and a pole with a Canadian flag, only slightly moving. Something about the place said it was the home of a bachelor, but one who was neat, self-sufficient and was used to a set routine.

It was a long time since Roberta had been inside, but she remembered it was tidily kept, with polished wood walls bearing photographs of Dan in his RCMP staff sergeant's uniform.

Through a window she could see Dan, wearing shorts and a tee shirt, sitting at the kitchen table reading a newspaper, his bare feet up on a chair. A cat was curled up on the floor, asleep. He was a tall, slim, fit, youthful man with a bronzed, finely-chiselled face and penetrating blue eyes.

When he heard Roberta's knock, he looked up, surprised that anyone should be visiting him this late at night.

"Hello, Sergeant!" Roberta said, grinning broadly, as he opened the door.

"Well, hello, Sergeant. I heard tell you were coming back, but I didn't know you had arrived."

They hugged warmly, Dan lifting her off her feet. Roberta brushed her lips against his cheek.

"Got here just before supper. You going to invite me in?"

"You bet! Come on and make yourself at home."

Roberta removed her sweater as Dan closed the door.

"Little Bobby! Let's have a good look at you." He looked her up and down, a little too appreciatively for Roberta's liking. "Sit down, sit down. You want a drink?"

"Sure, best offer I've had all day. What have you got?"

"By the look of it, I've got Scotch, Scotch and Scotch."

"In that case, I'll have Scotch." Roberta laughed, and Dan gave her a tender smile.

Outside the wind had risen and the clouds which had blocked the moon were now scudding across the sky. Small waves were appearing on the lake and were lapping at Dan's small jetty where his boat was rocking gently. The light from Dan's kitchen sent soft shafts across the newly-cut grass.

"You heard about our new celebrity neighbour, then?"

"Yes. You know, I used to watch his show every week for years. How old would he be now?"

"About my age, I guess," said Dan diffidently, as he was always conscious of his being years older than Roberta.

"What's he doing up here I wonder."

"Apparently, his acting career took a dive when *Hampton Nights* came to an end. I think the series ran for something like twelve years. I have no idea what he did between then and now. I guess he's retired...like me."

"How are you liking that?"

"Not bad. I like living around here. As you know, this used to be my vacation place. But ever since I retired I've been asking myself why in God's name I did. Tell you the truth, I miss the action. I loved that job."

"I know exactly what you mean. Couldn't be without mine."

"Still, I'm with the Fire Department, so I get some activity and excitement from time to time. Had some earlier today. It was just brush this time, fortunately, but you could tell it was deliberately set."

"Where was this?"

"Down by MacPhee's brook. Not a lot of damage done."

"How bad was it?" Roberta asked.

"Guy's shed and part of his garage."

Dan refilled their glasses. Roberta noted with satisfaction that Dan had graduated from the Johnnie Walker he used to serve to Glen Rothes, a huge improvement in her judgment.

"Rod tells me he has become a pillar of the community," said Roberta.

"Who?"

"John Sedgemoor."

"Oh yeah. On the committee at the Legion, heads up the cancer drive. Volunteer fireman. He's a regular guy. He's always helping out around the village. Everybody likes him."

"Why do I get the feeling you're not one of them?"

"Dunno. There's something about the guy that's too good to be true. Too smarmy."

"Maybe he's just too good-looking. Competition for you."

Dan grinned. "Nah. I'm in a league of my own."

"Ha! Tell me about Mrs. Sedgemoor."

"That's a whole other story! You have to meet her. She's foreign, for starters, German, I think. And she has very strange ways. Snooty and bad-tempered. Pretty near everybody hates her."

"Including you?"

"Oh yeah. I can't stand the cow."

Roberta laughed, guzzled down her drink, grabbed her sweater and got up. "I've got to be going. Rod is waiting up for me."

She leaned over and kissed his cheek.

Dan took her hand. "Come and see me again soon, Bobby."

"Sure will. Goodnight, Sergeant."

"Goodnight, Sergeant."

6: Speed bonny boat

The wind was up when Roberta left Dan's place, and the trees were tossing, making a loud rustling sound. Barely-visible dark clouds scurried rapidly through the sky, permitting only tiny, intermittent bursts of moonlight to appear. The water could be heard lashing against the shoreline, and Dan's boat was knock-knocking against the jetty.

After walking some yards, Roberta thought she heard a sounds of someone following her at a short distance. She stopped, turned round sharply and stared into the blackness. She could see and hear nothing, but when she started moving again, she thought she could hear the footsteps recommence.

Rapidly she strode up the hill to the Gillis house, and was almost running when she turned into the driveway and took the steps two at a time.

Rod was lying on the sofa, half asleep, half watching a late movie with the sound turned down.

"Sorry I took so long."

Rod stirred, stretched, sat up and peered at his watch. "Holy Mother! Did you ever. What the hell were you doing all this time?"

"Just gabbing."

"I've got to get to bed. I have to be at the Strait by seven. We'll have to finish our talk some other time."

He got up, switched off the television and stumbled wearily to the door. When he was half way through Roberta stopped him with a hand on his arm.

"What?" Rod asked impatiently.

"I think I was being followed tonight."

"Followed? How do you mean, followed? Who'd want to follow you?"

"It was on my way down to Dan's. I thought I saw someone spying on me."

"Spying on you?"

"Then again on the way back, I was sure somebody was coming up hill behind me."

"You're not in Toronto now. The crime rate around here is close to zero."

"Remember what Sherlock Holmes said about how the countryside hid more evil than all the cities."

"It's late, Bobby. You'd better get some sleep. You've had an awful long day."

"Maybe you're right," Roberta conceded, "I am

kind of bushed."

Rod headed for the stairs, muttering to himself: "Sherlock Holmes! Jesus!"

Roberta grinned and switched the lights off.

~

Sweaty and tangled up in a single sheet, Roberta was dead to the world when Rod entered, crept up and gave her a shake. He put a little alarm clock on the night table.

Roberta stirred and groggily opened one eye. "What's wrong?"

"I'm off to work. Don't forget you've got to get the kids off to school."

Roberta groaned assent, turned over and in an instant was asleep again.

Several hours later, the sun was up and streaming through the curtains. When the alarm rang, loud, harsh and grating, Roberta sat up in confusion. She peered around the unfamiliar surroundings, then struggled to turn off the clock.

She got up, went to the door, shouting, "Come on you lot! Up! Bonnie! Brad! Get your asses in gear!"

After much fussing and arguing, the three children were sat round the kitchen table. Bonnie and Brad were dressed, but Angie was still in her pajamas. Brad was sullen but ate everything which Roberta put in front of him.

She rushed around cooking, handing out plates, barking instructions, asking who wanted more toast, and telling them not to forget to take their school books with them.

Roberta bundled the two older children out of the front door just as the school bus was coming up the hill. When the children had climbed on board and Roberta waved to them, only Bonnie returned the wave.

"Who's that woman?" asked Bonnie's friend, Charlene.

"That's my aunt from Toronto. She's a cop."

"What do you mean, a cop?"

"She's a sergeant. A detective," Bonnie said proudly.

"A detective." Charlene snorted. "Yeah, right!"

Some other girls in nearby seats giggled. One of them nodded in Bonnie's direction and rolled her eyes.

~

The sky was virtually cloudless and the sun was already quite warm. Roberta and Angie sat on the back step, gazing out across the lakes and, except where the barn interceded, they had a clear view over to Morrison's Head and beyond to Johnstown and Irish Cove. Angie snuggled close to Roberta, who put her arm around her.

Roberta started to sing:

> *Speed bonnie boat, like a bird on the wing*
> *Onward! The sailors cry.*
> *Carry the lad that's born to be King*
> *Over the sea to Skye*

"Ooh, I know that one," cried Angie, joining in.

> *Loud the wind howls, loud the waves roar*
> *Thunderclaps rend the air*
> *Baffled, our foes stand on the shore*
> *Follow, they will not dare*
> *Speed bonnie boat, like a bird on the wing*
> *Onward! The sailors cry*
> *Carry the lad that's born to be King*
> *Over the sea to Skye*

The sound of a car horn interrupted their musical reverie.

"That's Mrs. MacLeod," said Angie, leaping up and running to the front yard. "'Bye, Aunty Bob!"

As Roberta watched Mrs. MacLeod's car go, Angie

and two other small children peered out of the back window. All three were waving to her. She watched the car for a few minutes, then when it had disappeared, went up to see to her mother.

Once she had dressed the old woman, she tried to feed her some breakfast but Mrs. Gillis was not interested, completely ignoring what was offered, so Roberta took a large brush and slowly, softly brushed her mother's long, white hair. As she worked she continued to sing *Speed Bonnie Boat*. If she liked Roberta's singing, or even heard it, she gave no sign of having done so.

7: Norman's store

There were not many stores left in the nation like Norman MacKenzie's, not even in the depth of the remotest countryside. A general store in every sense of the term, it had stout, shiny, wooden counters along the sides of the long, high-ceilinged, barn-like building, piled high with jars and large cans. Behind each counter were dozens of shelves crammed with dry goods, foodstuffs, hardware, patent medicine, rat poison, soap, detergent and other merchandise.

On the scrubbed and saw-dusted plank floor sat large wooden chests of tea, and barrels containing flour, seed and poultry feed. Hanging from the rafters were handsaws, stepladders, rubber hoses, skeins of twine, toilet plungers, axes, dog leashes, wooden rules, snow shovels, rakes and even a bicycle. Wherever there were spaces on the whitewashed walls, huge calendars competed with faded, old-fashioned posters for Pears soap, Alka-Seltzer, Sifta salt, Robin Hood flour, and Carter's little liver pills. In short, MacKenzie's was something of a museum as well as a store.

Norman, in his full white apron, leant across the counter, gossiping with local resident Violet McIntosh. Norman's wife, Gertie, scurried around, checking lists, re-arranging items, and putting stock on shelves. It was clear that, in this emporium, Norman did most of the talking while Gertie did most of the work.

Roberta needed a few household items, but dropped by the store more to renew old acquaintances and refresh her memories. After all, Norman's store was more like a community centre than a shop, being the place where most news and gossip were exchanged, and where many locals, especially seniors, came to sit on the old barrels and tell yarns.

"Hello, Norman, hello, Gertie," she said as she poked her head round the door. "Long time, no see."

"Bobby Gillis, well I do declare!" Norman boomed, a great smile on his face, while Gertie came from behind the counter and vigorously hugged her.

"My dear, Roberta," said Gertie, "It's some lovely to see you after all this time."

"And looking good, too," said Norman.

Gertie gave him a sharp glance, so Norman quickly turned to the list Roberta had pushed across the counter, and busied himself with finding the items on the shelves behind him.

"Sorry to hear about Shirley," said Gertie. "It was a terrible shock for all of us."

"Yes, just awful. I'm so sorry for your troubles," Violet chimed in.

"And Violet!" Roberta turned to the older woman. "I haven't seen you in such a long time. I do hope you're keeping well."

"Tolerably well," said Violet. "I must say it is a tonic to see you blooming. That Toronto must agree with you, though I couldn't live in that place for love nor money."

"It has its pluses and minuses," Roberta said, "like anywhere else, I guess."

At that moment the doorbell rang and another neighbour, Ida Ferguson, entered. Ida had been a great favourite of Roberta's in days gone by, and she had always thought that Ida had a rough tongue but a good heart. She noticed that the older woman had aged considerably since she had last seen her, and somehow appeared down at heel.

Ida squinted at Roberta in amazement. "My heavens! Bobby Gillis. Come here and let me see if it is really you. My eyes are not what they used to be."

They embraced warmly, and Ida stroked her as if she were a family pet. "Sorry for your troubles, my dear. Shirley was well liked around here."

"Thank you. That's very kind of you to say so," said Roberta. "It's lovely to see you, Ida. I must come up to see you one of those days."

"Yes, girl, please do that. I imagine I could find a cup of tea for you."

Norman placed Roberta's purchases and the list on the counter. "Thirty-two dollars and fifty three cents, Bobby."

Roberta dug in her purse and counted out the money. "Well, I must be going," she said, "It was wonderful to see you all again."

They all said their goodbyes at the same time, the result sounding like something from the parrot cage at a zoo.

Roberta slipped out the door and headed up the hill.

"Well," said Gertie, "who'd have thought it? Roberta come home again after all this time."

"It will be good to have her around," said Ida.

"Such a lovely girl," Violet said. "She was always such a well behaved child."

"She'll add a little glamour to the place, that's for sure," Norman said a little too enthusiastically.

"You, get going," Gertie snapped like a garter belt. "Go get them supplies, pronto!"

8: The MacDonalds

Later, Roberta casually sauntered up the hill, appreciatively observing her surroundings and gently humming to herself. She bent down to retrieve a large maple leaf, already yellow, which had blown off a tree.

By a bend in the road, she paused to take in the spectacular view of the twinkling lakes basking in the morning sun. A far-distant boat was making its way towards Grand Narrows, and on the other side there came a momentary flash as a car roof reflected the sunlight.

As she was marvelling at the beauties of nature, a shadow fell over her. Someone seized her from behind, putting both arms around her and pressing her tightly to his body.

Roberta let out a cry. Then, using her police training, she twisted free, swung round and landed a sharp kick to the man's belly. He fell heavily to the ground with a loud groan of anguish.

Now in attack position, Roberta darted forward, but stopped dead when he saw the man's face. It was Randy MacDonald.

"Randy! You stupid bastard!"

Randy was a naturally-arrogant, extremely well-developed, devilishly-handsome man in his early thirties. Like a predatory animal, he was in the prime of condition, everything about him exuding sensuality.

"Jesus, Bobby, don't kill me."

"Randy, you are an idiot. You scared the life out of me."

Reaching out to take his hand, Roberta pulled him to his feet.

He was wearing very tight jeans and an abbreviated T-shirt which showed off his superb physique. Perspiration was shining on his muscles and in places was staining the shirt. "I just wanted to cop a quick feel to welcome you home," he said with a pronounced leer.

"You don't ever change, do you?" Roberta punched his arm, then gave him a hug. "Your brains are still in your pants."

"You don't fancy a few brains, right now, do you, Bobby?"

"God, you're bad. Always were, always will be."

"Well, maybe I am. You're looking awful good, girl,

but I can tell you're not getting much," he said making a lunge for her.

"Not like you, I'll bet," said Roberta as she pushed him away.

"Oh, they keep me pretty busy," said Randy with a conceited grin. "There's an awful lot of hungry women around here."

He reached out and stroked her arm. "But I can always find time to fit you in. How about behind them bushes over there?"

Roberta slapped the hand away and darted out of his reach. "I was just coming up to see your people. Are they home?"

"Sure are. Come on up."

They strolled up the hill, making their way to an old, weather-beaten wreck of a farm house on the high side of a muddy dirt track. Before they reached the track, they passed a large house, the old Ferguson place.

Roberta noticed *Sedgemoor* on a mailbox at the side of the road. Curious, she stopped for a minute, staring at the house and searching for signs of life around the property. Seeing none, she moved on.

"See you're interested in our movie star," said Randy. "Leastways, that's what they say. I can't remember seeing him in any movies."

"That's because you're too young."

"Yeah, but I got nothing against older women, Bobby."

"Get going," she commanded, pushing him up the road. "You're a sex maniac."

~

The MacDonald house had not been repaired or painted in many decades and gave the impression of being ready to collapse at a moment's notice. Indeed the entire scene which faced Roberta as she came upon it was reminiscent of a Disney cartoon movie, all of the outbuildings looking as if they should have fallen down long ago and were being held up by magic.

The yard was filled with debris of all descriptions, decaying old car bodies, ancient tractors, rotting wagons, piles of warped, grey planks, tires, boxes, rusty pipes, dilapidated lobster traps, piles of manure, old barrels, bicycle frames, and discarded tools all competing for the limited space available. Through this extraordinary landscape innumerable dogs, cats, chickens and geese aimlessly wandered. A shaggy old horse tried to graze on a balding patch of grass and, nearby, a pair of loudly bleating goats was tethered.

As Roberta and Randy picked their way through

this shambles, they narrowly escaped being hit by a shovelful of manure which came hurtling out of a cowshed doorway.

"Whoa, Skit!" Randy shouted. "Hold up!"

A face peered around the doorway, and then a curious figure came towards them. Skit was a man of indeterminate age in whom some kind of disability caused him to lurch from side to side as he walked, his face permanently twisted into a weird grin. Roberta remembered that he also had great difficulty in speaking and being understood, tending to drop the first letter of certain words. He was dressed in odd, ill-assorted clothes he must have picked up around the village, including a bizarre cotton shirt which had *Kiss Me. I'm a Virgin* printed on the chest. His arms, legs and boots were spattered with manure.

He loped towards them.

"Hello Skit," said Roberta. "Remember me?"

"Uh-uh. 'Obby."

"That's right. Bobby. How are you getting along?"

"Good 'Obby. 'Ow're you?"

"I'm great. You working hard?"

"Oh yes. 'Ucking out the cowshed. I'd 'etter get 'ack to it."

"See you later, Skit," said Roberta.

Skit bobbed and weaved back into the shed, and

immediately manure began to fly again.

"He hasn't changed."

"No, poor bastard. He's got a heart of gold and works like a slave."

"Do you pay him like a slave?" Roberta asked, a little snottily.

"He's got his pension. I got no idea what he does with it. We don't pay him much but he gets a place to sleep and all his grub. He's okay."

"Where does he sleep, in the barn?" Roberta was surprised to hear herself being so censorious.

"No, in the house, of course," said Randy. "But Grampy Linus still has his place in back of the barn."

"He still going strong?"

"Oh yeah. Still as cranky as ever. Ninety-one, he is now. He can't walk, not even a few steps, but he's still sharp as a tack."

As they climbed the rickety front steps of the house, Roberta noticed that the door, whitened with age, was hanging by one hinge. Fastened to it was a tattered wreath, obviously from many Christmases ago.

A smell, not entirely unpleasant, assailed her as they walked through to the kitchen. She could not put her finger on the identity of the odour, but she became aware of an intense atmosphere of animal fecundity and latent sexuality, making her unusually warm and slightly uncomfortable.

A litter of tiny kittens nestled with their mother just inside the door, and a hugely pregnant bitch sprawled under the table. Everywhere there were bowls of eggs, shiny fruit, fat, suggestive cucumbers, gleaming tomatoes, pillowy loaves of bread, and bulging potatoes. Hanging from the rafters were a plump chicken, a bunch of enormous carrots, a glistening, fat smoked ham, and clusters of pungent herbs.

Dangling at random among the comestibles were items of female underwear, some commodious and utilitarian, others scant, sheer and frilly. On nails and hooks on the walls hung all manner of pots, pans and utensils. On top of a huge, old-fashioned fridge, a small radio quietly played country and western music.

Roberta noticed that all the furniture was wooden, old, worn and solid, almost all of it occupied by sleek, contented well-fed animals.

"Look what the cat dragged in, Ma," said Randy. "It's little Bobby Gillis."

Lolly MacDonald was at the table, rolling dough, while her daughter, Lavender, stretched out on the couch, filing her nails and sharing the space with a large ginger cat. Lolly was a large, extremely buxom, roly-poly woman in her early fifties. She had bright, merry eyes, shiny red apple cheeks, and moist, red lips usually parted in a smile or a laugh. Her long, ash-streaked hair was tied back with a rubber band. Her big arms were covered in flour which, when she wiped the perspiration off her brow, she transferred to her face.

"My Lord! Bobby Gillis!" cried Lolly. "You're looking awful good, Bobby."

"That's what I was telling her just now," said Randy. "I asked if she wanted a quickie, but she weren't interested."

Lolly and Lavender cackled with laughter, so loudly it scared one of the cats, which darted off under a cabinet.

"I can see you folks are alright," Roberta said. "You still breaking hearts, Lavender?"

"Breaking backs more like," hooted Randy.

Again, Lolly and Lavender laughed uproariously.

"Don't pay no mind to him," said Lavender. "He's just jealous I got a better love life than him!"

Rebecca took a good look at Lavender, a lively, mischievous woman of about thirty who looked rather like a *Penthouse* model. She was almost as tall as her brother, with big, wandering blue eyes, short blonde hair, and pouting pink lips. She wore abbreviated, scarlet shorts and a white, tight, lightweight, short sleeved sweater at least one size too small for her.

"Like a pair of rabbits, they are, Bobby," said Lolly, "and me trying to be respectable. What's a decent, God-fearing woman to do?"

"Oh yeah?" Randy interjected, "Ask her about that commercial traveller fellow that come through here, selling knives and stuff!"

"Oh, you shush, now!" Lolly was flustered.

"And she's got the hots for that Sedgemoor down the road here," said Lavender.

"She's not the only one," Randy said. "You said yourself, Lavvy, that you'd like to put your shoes under his bed."

"He is kind of cute, but he's too old for me. Got lovely manners, though." She gave Randy a knowing look. "Not like some I could mention."

"So, Sedgemoor is too old for you, is he? That Gordie MacNeil weren't too old for you after the Legion dance the other week. And him damn near sixty!"

"You shut your mouth. You know Gordie's different. He's been a regular from way back."

They all laughed, Lolly shaking like a jelly.

"Speaking of manners," Lolly said, "take some stuff with you. I got a basket all made for old Mrs. McPhee, but I can easy do another one for her. The tomaters are the best we ever had."

She handed Roberta the basket, brimming with good things including, she noticed, a lovely-smelling loaf of freshly-made bread.

"Thanks a million, Lolly. I'll just look in on old Linus, then I'll be on my way."

"He'll be glad to see you. Don't be a stranger now!"

Roberta left by the back door and picked her way through the yard, swishing away a flock of chickens and two hissing geese, until she got to the lean-to hut against the back of the barn. In order to get to the door, she had to navigate around precarious stacks of old tires and boxes, taking care not to knock anything over. Peering through the cracked, misted, little window pane, she could see Linus sitting in his old rocking chair.

"Linus! It's me, Bobby Gillis," Roberta called out as she knocked on the door. "Are you decent?"

"Bobby Gillis? Holy Jesus. Come on in, girl, come on in!"

She opened the creaky, old door and poked her head inside. She was almost overcome by 'old man' smell, but persisted and perched herself on the edge of a cluttered counter.

The hut was squalid, overflowing with all manner of bric-a-brac, books, newspapers, and girly magazines. On the walls were pinned an out-of-date calendar and several *Playboy* centrefolds.

"My heavens!" cried Linus, "you're looking right some beautiful, girl. A sight for sore eyes, and no mistake."

He was a small, spare man with a gleaming bald head with small tufts of white hair around his ears. His eyes shone with excitement, his cheeks red and shiny, and when he smiled he revealed a set of irregular, yellowing teeth. Roberta noticed that Linus spoke in a more 'Scotchy' country accent than the others, almost exhibiting the lisp which Cape Bretoners call 'buckish'.

He reached over and patted her knee. "Come and have a little cuddle, Bobby."

"Linus! At your age, too!"

"I can't walk, but everything else is in working order." He cackled like an old hen. "There may be snow on the roof, but there's still fire in the furnace."

"You're impossible, the lot of you! Anyway, I've got to go. I just wanted to say hello."

"Okay. But there's many a good tune played on an old fiddle, you know."

"I'm going before I get to be part of some scandal. Goodbye, Linus."

"See you, Bobby. I'm sorry for your troubles, you and Rod, Shirley was a fine woman, no mistake."

"Thanks, Linus. I'll see you around."

~

When Roberta turned off the MacDonalds' trackway onto the road, she wandered over to the look-off and gazed out across the expanse of water. To her left she spied the Cameron Island lighthouse, and George Island beyond it. Far away on the other shore she could just see the little village of Red Islands and behind it the relatively high ground of Mount Auburn. The distant woods were beginning their change from green to lemon. To her left were Dumpling Island, the twin Crammond Islands and Floda Island, and just ahead she could see a cluster of eight more small islands.

She remembered their names because she had known them since she was a child when she and her friends had chanted, *Green, Clarke, Cow, Rook, Calf, Low, McRae's, Ranald*. All were now speckled with flashes of yellow from their turning trees. There was some haze at this time of day, but if she used her imagination, she could discern the Barra Strait away to the east, and the big bridge at Grand Narrows and Iona.

In the harbour, down at Marble Mountain, some men were doing something—she couldn't tell what—to a blue boat; two of them actually working, two more looking on. She remembered her father telling her that marble had been quarried at the now small, peaceful community since the 1880s, and that at its peak some seven hundred workers were employed there.

In those far off days, he had told her, Marble Mountain had an Oddfellows Hall, posh homes, a three-room schoolhouse, half a dozen stores, two churches, a hotel and a bank. Following the First World War it all came to an end, and Marble Mountain gradually reverted to a quiet village of around seventy souls.

The air was clean and fresh, but slightly chilly, and she wished she had brought a sweater. She became aware of something strange in her back pocket and, digging it out, found it was a Presto Toronto subway ticket. Toronto seemed so very far away now, another country, certainly another time.

In a field close by, she noticed a hare nibbling at some vegetation, its giant hind legs making it look like a miniature kangaroo. Two crows were swooping and diving overhead. Somewhere, unseen, a bull was bellowing at the top of its lungs.

Roberta did not see that, some yards across the road, a man was on his knees, tinkering with a mower on the lawn in front of the house. Straightening up, he noticed her in the distance, and, tossing his wrench on the grass, leisurely strolled towards her. He was very tall, about fifty, with a handsome, preternaturally youthful face, twinkling eyes, and an incipient smile playing about his lips.

She was too engrossed in her surroundings to hear his approach, so when he spoke she was taken by surprise.

"Good afternoon." His voice was a rich baritone.

Startled, she whirled around, spilling the contents of her basket on the ground.

"Oh. Hello," she said, just staring at him, feeling an instant attraction which embarrassed her and made her blush.

"Sorry about that," he said. "My fault entirely for taking you unawares. I'm John Sedgemoor."

"I know. I used to watch you when I was a kid."

"I prefer to take that as meaning that you're still very young," said Sedgemoor with a smile. He stooped down to pick up the items spilled from her basket.

Over his shoulder Roberta saw a woman's face appear at one of the front windows, a face apparently not liking what it saw.

"I'm sorry, I don't understand."

"The alternative being that I should be in a museum," Sedgemoor laughed.

"Oh, Mr. Sedgemoor I didn't mean it like that," Roberta stuttered. "I meant that I was a teenager... well...almost twenty."

"Call me John, please. And you are...?"

The woman at the window had come out on to the front step and was standing there with her arms folded. She was an overweight, sour-looking person in her late fifties. She glared at Roberta with obvious disapproval.

"Roberta Gillis," she said.

"Ah yes. You're Rod's sister, the detective."

"I guess I am."

"Johan!" shouted the woman from the step. "Come here. I want you!"

A flicker of annoyance, possibly distaste, flashed across his face, but in an instant the smile had returned.

"Right away, Lutzi!" he called to the woman. Then to Roberta he said: "I'd better go and see what The Warden wants. Please come and see me again sometime...soon."

"I will."

"Johan! Johan!" the woman bawled again.

"Goodbye," said Sedgemoor, giving her the slightest trace of a wink.

~

Just as Roberta was turning into the front driveway, Mrs. MacLeod's car pulled up. Angie tumbled out, ran to Roberta and hugged her around the legs. She waved goodbye to Mrs. MacLeod, and watched until the car was out of sight.

"Hello, my poppet. Did you have a good day at school?"

"Not really, Aunty Bob. Some of the girls were asking me about Mommy." She started to weep. "I don't want to talk about Mommy. Not to them."

"I understand, pet," said Roberta, picking her up. "They'll soon lose interest and stop bothering you."

"I hope they will."

"Tell you what. Let's go and see if there's any ice cream in the fridge."

"Okay," said Angie, brightening up. "Can I carry your basket for you?"

"Sure. It's kind of heavy, so be careful."

She put Angie down gently and passed her the basket, which the little girl dragged along the ground and bumped up the steps to the front door.

"Did you have a good day, Aunty Bob?"

"Yes thank you, Sweetie," Roberta said thoughtfully. "I think I did have a good day."

~

Later that evening, Roberta and Rod were sitting on the couch, Rod buried in his newspaper, his sister watching television. Brad and Angie had gone to bed, but through the open door Bonnie could be seen doing her homework at the kitchen table.

Rod suddenly looked up. "I guess you heard about the fire."

"Yes, Dan told me about it the other night."

"No, this was today at Blacky Chisholm's place."

"I didn't know. When was this?"

From the kitchen, Bonnie called out, "Charlene was saying about it on the 'phone. I forgot to tell you."

"This evening," said Rod. "I saw it on my way home."

"Much damage?"

"Not that I could see. Maybe a chicken coop." Rod returned to his newspaper.

Roberta looked at her watch. "Time to pack it in, Bonnie. It's late."

"Yeah okay. I'm just finishing up."

"How's work?" Roberta asked Rod.

"Mmm?"

"The job. How's it coming along?"

"Not bad. If this weather holds we may even be ahead of schedule."

"That's good. I called about Ma today."

"Oh, yeah. What did they say?"

"There's a long waiting list," said Roberta, "but

when I explained the circumstances, they said we might be able to jump the queue."

"That sounds encouraging. Did they say where?"

"Either Baddeck or the Strait. I said the Strait would be better. Is that right?"

"Yeah, it's closer and a lot of my jobs are down around there, so I could look in on her more often. When will they let us know?"

"In a few weeks, they said."

Rod went back to his newspaper, then a few minutes later he folded it and put it on the side table. "Have you thought any more about staying longer, Bobby?"

"Longer than a month, you mean?"

"Yeah."

"I've been thinking about it. You know I can't give up my career, but I will give serious consideration to trying to get more time."

"Thanks Bobby. I really appreciate it."

Roberta got up to stretch her legs and wandered to the front porch, stretching and breathing deeply. A cool breeze was blowing off the lakes, but the sky was clear and the stars were out in force. Sirius and Canopus were bright and clear, and she thought she could identify Jupiter and Saturn, but she was not so sure about Mars because it was so faint.

Ever so quietly a small, white-tailed doe had

emerged from the long shadows on the front lawn and was nibbling at the flower beds. An owl had started hooting somewhere nearby. Everything seemed amazingly peaceful.

When the deer looked up suddenly and darted away, it drew Roberta's attention to the trees on the other side of the road. This time there was no question about it: somebody was standing in the shadows of a large pine tree.

Hurriedly, she slipped inside and ran to the living room. "Rod, he's here again. Right across the road."

"What? Who?" Rod seemed annoyed at being disturbed.

"Whoever followed me last night. He's here again."

Rod leapt out of his chair, grabbed a flashlight from the hall stand and tore out of the house. He bounded down the steps and, shining the light across the road, ran to the other side.

Roberta watched him as he searched around, the flashlight weirdly flickering on the tree trunks. Rod even walked some way up and then down the hill, searching for a putative watcher, but with no apparent success.

The light went out and Rod returned to the front steps.

"Well?" Roberta asked anxiously.

"There's nobody there."

"Well, he was there. I'm sure of it."

"You're the detective, Sis. Why don't you have a poke around tomorrow when there's more light. If there was someone there, maybe they left some trace." He grinned broadly. "Isn't that what Sherlock Holmes would do?"

"Smart ass!"

"You want me to put crime scene tape around it?"

"I'll put a tape on your mouth if you don't stop. This is serious."

"Well, there's nothing we can do about it tonight," Rod said, "except lock all the doors. Come on, Bobby: let's hit the hay."

9: Lutzi

The next morning was cool and cloudy, with a few early leaves blowing along the road, and the smaller birds appearing to be tossed about by the wind.

After she had dispatched all the children to school, Roberta put on her jeans, wind-breaker and rubber boots and crossed the road. She carried a bamboo cane and several clear plastic bags. She negotiated the ditch, clambered up the bank into the trees and, using the cane to lift the fallen leaves and prod aside twigs, stones and grass, began her search.

At the top of a grassy bank encroaching on a patch of dogwood, and close to the boughs of the pines, Roberta gently but thoroughly examined a patch of grass which some creature had clearly trampled, but whether animal or human she could not determine. Continuing the search, she came across a rusty old can which must have been discarded many years ago, but little else.

Frustrated, she straightened up and stared into

the woods. Frowning, she suddenly smelled something—she couldn't say what—that seemed out of place.

Looking down, all she could see was grass with what looked like mud stains on it. She knelt down, put her nose very close to the grass and sniffed.

So preoccupied with her task was she, that Roberta did not notice John Sedgemoor walking up the hill in her direction. Still unable to place the smell, she crawled forward, furiously sniffing.

When John drew level with her he stopped quietly and, obviously amused, stood observing her. In the crook of his arm he carried a white rabbit. "Are you hunting for truffles?"

Roberta almost jumped out of her skin, overcome with embarrassment. Her face was suffused with red. "Oh, it's you. What did you say?"

"I asked if you were hunting for truffles. That's the way pigs do it in France."

"Thanks a million for the comparison."

Very self-consciously Roberta stood up, brushing leaves and grass off her jeans. "Do you make a habit of coming up on people when they're not looking?"

"Sorry."

"I was...er...um...it's a long story," she said.

"But a fascinating one, no doubt," said John.

"I may tell you about it someday. What a cute rabbit. Is it yours?”

“No, it belongs to little Margie MacAskill.”

Roberta scrambled down the bank, jumped the ditch, and joined him on the road. She gently stroked the rabbit.

“Be careful,” John cautioned. “The unfortunate creature has a broken leg.”

“Aww, poor bunny. What are you going to do with it? You’re not going to put it down?”

“If I tell you, do you promise not to turn me in for practising without a veterinary license?”

“You’re going to fix the leg?” Roberta sounded incredulous.

“Yep. I’m going to re-set the bone and put it in a cast. If you walk up to the house with me you can as-sist in the operation.”

“Yes, I’d love to.”

They started to saunter on up the hill towards John’s house.

“The MacAskills can’t easily get to a vet, and in any case they don’t have the money to pay for one. They know I go in for this kind of thing, so they asked me to help. I was only too glad to oblige.”

“I think that’s wonderful!” Roberta surprised her-self by the degree of enthusiasm in her voice.

On one side of the Sedgemoors’ house was a se-ries of hutches and cages in which a variety of animals hobbled and fluttered about, each one having some kind of disability. In one cage, a crow with a broken wing carked at them. In another was a squirrel with a bandaged leg. In a third was a cat with a dressing over its eye.

"This is a regular hospital," Roberta exclaimed. "Holy cow!"

"No, no cows," John laughed. "I'm not equipped to handle large animals."

"Are there many calls upon your veterinary skills?"

"I do what I can to help them. Sometimes the poor things are beyond hope, but I have a reasonable success rate so far."

"Where did you learn this?"

"I picked it up here and there. I grew up on a farm." John handed the rabbit to Roberta. "Let's take care of this little fellow. If you'll hold him for a minute, I'll get my equipment."

Roberta gingerly accepted the rabbit and, with something approaching awe, watched him disappear into the house. When he returned they sat on the top of the back steps while John performed his procedure.

He put the finishing touches to the cast and passed the creature back to Roberta. "There. That should do it. Will you hold him still until the plaster dries?"

"Sure."

"Keep him very still. Don't let him wriggle around if you can avoid it."

John replaced his things in an old leather bag and sat back, relaxing.

"Tell me," said Roberta. "I was wondering what happened to you after *Hampton Nights*. I didn't see you in anything after that."

"Sad story. I got a few parts. Unfortunately, nothing of any consequence. By that time I was too typecast as the English butler. You see, I went to America with my parents when I was seventeen, so I had the accent naturally until my late twenties and thirties. But towards the end of *Hampton Nights* I had become a North American and was losing it, so I was having to fake the voice. Then, after the series was canned, I guess I didn't have any distinctive marketable quality."

"But you were such a good actor."

"Not really. An Englishman doesn't have to be that good to play an English butler. You just have to give Americans the stereotype they expect."

"That is rather sad," Roberta said.

"Contrary to what the Americans believe, there is probably only a small handful of real butlers left in England, and I doubt if many of those spoke with a plummy, cut-glass accent. Most of them likely have working-class accents. The Jeeves type disappeared in the thirties."

"I hadn't realized that."

"Ah, well, that's all blood under the bridge now. How is Br'er Rabbit doing?"

"I think the cast has set now."

"Good."

John gently took the rabbit and transferred it to an empty cage. "Let's go in and have a cup of coffee. You'll get to meet Lutzi." He gave her a strange, con-spiratorial look and, she thought, maybe a hint of wink. "I'll bet that will be an education for you."

As they went in through the back door, John paused to slip off his shoes. Roberta felt obliged to follow suit.

"Don't mind Lutzi," he said in an undertone. "She has some strange ways...and a singular sense of humour."

They came into the kitchen, which was magnifi-cently appointed with state-of-the-art appliances and equipment. Shining copper cookware, knives and ladles hung from strategically placed hooks. Roberta watched John in this space, and immediately formed the impression that he did the cooking in this establishment, and that he took it very seriously.

Bundles of fresh herbs sat in vases of water, and

on the huge counter was a large basket of fresh mushrooms of various shapes and colours.

Roberta went over to examine them. The sight somehow reminded her of old paintings of country village fairs and weddings. "Ooh, look at these! Are they wild?"

"Well, they're not very happy," said John with a grin. Roberta heard herself giggling like a little girl. "Yes, they are all from the woods around here."

"They're beautiful. How do you know which ones are good and which ones are the bad guys?"

"Experience mostly. Trial and error to some extent."

"Trial and error!" said Roberta "That doesn't sound very appealing."

"It isn't. I ended up in intensive care once and took two friends with me. A good time was *not* had by all. Still, that was when I was young and foolish, about a hundred years ago. It never happened again —I made sure of that. I guess I'm what you could call an expert mycologist now. There's an old saying that there are old mycologists and there are bold mycologists, but there are no old, bold mycologists."

Roberta heard herself giggle again. Then she asked, "Do you go picking every day?"

"A few times a week, usually. It depends on the weather."

"The weather? How does the weather affect your picking? Can't you pick in the rain?"

"No, nothing like that. It's just that, in a long dry spell, you'll see hardly any mushrooms, but after a real downpour you can expect a good harvest."

"Could I go with you when you go out next?"

"Sure. That would be my pleasure," John said. "We'll go out on Saturday."

"Thank you."

"I'd better give Lutzi a shout. I expect she's upstairs."

He stuck his head around the doorway. "Lutzi, darling! I've brought somebody to see you!"

To Roberta, he said, "Sit yourself down and make yourself comfortable. I'll put the coffee on."

As John was preparing the coffee, a large, forbidding woman entered the kitchen. She stopped, glared at Roberta and scowled.

"There you are dear," said John. "Lutzi, I'd like you to meet Roberta Gillis."

"Hello," Roberta said shyly.

"So! You have brought her here!" Lutzi said in a strong Germanic accent. "Is this shameless? There is no shame!"

John chuckled loudly. "Roberta's been helping me fix a rabbit with a broken leg."

"Pfff! Rabbits! Foolishness!" Lutzi spluttered.

Turning directly to Roberta she asked, "What are you? Are you a whore?"

Roberta was totally stunned, highly embarrassed and not knowing how to react.

John burst into a hearty laugh. "No, she's not a whore, my dear. She's a policewoman."

"Police? Hmph! What do the police want with me?"

"Roberta is a neighbour, Lutzi. Roberta is Rod Gillis's sister. You know they live just down the road."

"Gillis? What is this Gillis?" Lutzi exclaimed. "How can I be expected to remember all these names in my condition?"

Lutzi appeared to be undecided for a second, then, perhaps glad of an audience, she sat across from Roberta, addressing her in an almost confidential fashion. "I am a very sick woman. I have many, many serious complaints, but medical knowledge has hardly progressed at all. Did you know that?"

"No, I didn't. I'm sorry to hear you are unwell," said Roberta sincerely.

"What do you know?" Lutzi snorted. "You know nothing of the way I suffer. Here, the doctors are all fools!"

John set out the coffee things on the table, then returned to see if the kettle was boiling. When it did, he carefully poured water through the filter.

"In Europe it is different," Lutzi pronounced. "There one can find good specialists—real specialists. But here? Pfff! They are fools!"

"This is a lovely house, Mrs. Sedgemoor," said Roberta, anxious to change the subject. "You and John have done wonders with this old property, I remember how it used to be when the Fergusons had it."

Lutzi looked at her with a sneer and waved her hand dismissively. "This! What do you know! You know nothing. This is—what do you call it..?"

"A slum?" John volunteered.

"*Ja!* A slum. Exactly! You should have seen my family's estate in Austria. We had servants. And horses. And peacocks. And hunting dogs. We only spoke High German in our home. None of that coarse Low German you hear in the streets. And the house was very beautiful. Everything was the very best that money could buy."

"You must miss it," said Roberta kindly.

"*Ja*, I do miss it, I miss it with great pain." She looked around disdainfully. "*Und* now I am stuck here in this...what do you say...?"

"Boondocks," John said, "Middle of nowhere."

"*Ja*! Boondocks! Middle of nowhere. Stuck with him. With that. With Johan."

"Coffee's ready," announced John. He carried it to the table and, before he put it down, gave Lutzi an affectionate kiss on the cheek.

"Pfff!" she snorted, and sniffed her coffee suspiciously.

They sat in awkward silence for several minutes as Lutzi examined Roberta in a patronizing way. First, she peered disdainfully at Roberta's stockinged feet, then slowly, scornfully, minutely scrutinized every inch of her. This made Roberta feel extremely uncomfortable, and her face reddened.

"Well, I must go now, Mrs. Sedgemoor," she said, jumping up.

"And we must check on that rabbit," said John, belatedly coming to the rescue.

"*Ja, ja,*" said Lutzi dismissively. "Go see your stupid rabbits. Go! Go!"

Once in the yard, John looked at Roberta and grinned broadly. "What do you think of Lutzi?"

"I don't know what to think. I'm kind of..."

"Flabbergasted?"

"Well...kind of...I guess. Flabbergasted is one way to describe it."

"She has that effect on people," said John, "Don't worry about it. It's not just you."

"Is she really joking when she says those...outrageous things?"

"I've often wondered about that." John looked thoughtful. "I don't think she is. I think she means every word."

"Sickness does strange things to some people," said Roberta.

"Roberta, there's absolutely nothing wrong with her. Nothing. She's been to see dozens of doctors. None of them can find a thing."

"Really? And all that stuff about Austria and servants. Is that true?"

"Your guess is as good as mine," John said sadly. "I've never met them, or even seen photographs of them."

Bewildered, Roberta just stared at him, at a loss for words.

"I told you it would be an education for you, didn't I?" John said. "Well, I'll leave you to walk home by yourself. I must get back to the Warden."

"OK. Thanks. It's been...."

"An education?"

"Yes," Roberta said with a laugh, "it was that, alright."

10: Fire

Roberta wandered on down the road, baffled by what she had witnessed. One question kept nagging at her: How on earth did a lovely, sensible man like John get together with a thoroughly unpleasant and utterly weird woman like Lutzi? It made no sense on any level.

What a waste, she thought.

The only conclusion she could come to was that John had been down and out after *Hampton Nights* and that Lutzi had rescued him financially. But that would mean John was a not-very-nice opportunist, something she was very reluctant to accept.

She was now halfway home, walking past a hay field on the MacDonald property, when noises attracted her attention. Looking into the field she saw, not far away, that the tall grass was moving wildly.

Mindful of her nocturnal experiences, she cried out, "You can't hide! I know you're there!"

Suddenly, Roberta was confronted by the naked

figures of Randy and a young woman standing up in the hay.

"We ain't hiding, Bobby. Come and join us if you want."

The young woman giggled and ducked down out of sight.

Roberta shook her head, waved disdainfully and walked away. Randy's laughter followed her.

A little further down the hill, just past the Mac-Donald farm, Roberta turned a bend in the road and saw a column of smoke rising in the middle distance. From her vantage point it looked as if the smoke could be coming from the Gillis place.

"Oh no!' she cried. Panicking and breaking into a run, she charged headlong down the hill.

Rushing round another bend, Roberta almost collided with a cluster of irregularly parked cars and trucks, including a fire truck. Some way off the road a group of men were putting out a fire in the bush.

She flashed a glance at the Gillis house, some twenty metres away, and was greatly relieved that everything appeared normal.

She noticed Dan among the workers and called out to him. "Dan! How bad is it?"

"Just a little one," he shouted back. "Nothing we can't handle."

He scrambled down to the road and joined her.

"How're you doing Sergeant?"

"Not bad, thanks, Sergeant. How did this one get started?"

"Another mystery. Come on, I'll walk you home. These guys have got everything under control."

"Where's your car?" asked Roberta.

"I got a ride up with Cletus Lynch."

"Okay."

They sauntered on down the hill. The sun was sinking fast and a brisk breeze was rising, riffling through the trees. A murmuration of starlings swooped past high above them, their myriad wings an almost liquid, humming mass.

"I was surprised Sedgemoor didn't answer the fire call," said Dan.

"John? I was just with him up above. He didn't mention a fire call."

"John? Hmm. You must have spent some time with him, then?" Dan's voice had a slightly hostile edge.

"Sure. And I met the famous Lutzi."

"Did you, by God? What was your impression of her?"

"I can't make up my mind."

They turned in at the Gillis place and sat on the stoop.

"You must have had a wild time then if you met her. Norma MacKenzie calls her *The Mad Woman of*

Lime Hill."

"Yes, she was really weird, alright."

"What did you think of *him*?" Dan asked, somewhat tentatively.

"Oh, I really like him!" Roberta said. Then, realizing she sounded too enthusiastic, she added, "I mean, he's a nice-enough sort of guy. You know…interesting."

"Interesting huh?" Dan stood up. "I must be off. Are you going to drop by tonight?"

"If I can, when the kids are settled."

"Alright. See you, Sergeant."

"Yep. See you, Sergeant."

11: Take the flashlight

They were sitting around the table finishing their casserole supper, the remains of which were being fought over by Bonnie and Brad. Rod pushed his plate away. "She really called you a whore?"

"That's right," Roberta replied, laughing. Imitating Lutzi, she continued, "'What are you? Are you a whore?'"

"Unbelievable!" said Rod.

"That's what I thought. You could have knocked me down with a feather."

"Daddy," piped up Angie. "What's a whore?"

"I'll tell you later," said Bonnie.

"You will do no such thing!" Rod was adamant. "Now get busy, you lot. You've all got homework to do."

"I don't got homework, Daddy."

"Yes, I know, sweetie. You go and watch television."

The children scrambled down and dispersed

throughout the house. Roberta piled the dirty dishes in the sink and then started to wash them.

From the table, Rod watched her. She was a different person from the one he had grown up with, different even from the last time she had visited Lime Hill, two years ago. He wondered what and where she would be now, had she not gone to Police College and then moved away from the district. She could not have stayed around here, that's for sure, he thought.

There were few opportunities in the rural parts of Cape Breton even for the uneducated, and Bobby had always been the smart one. She could never have been content with being a waitress or a store employee. When he had been tearing off to ball games and hockey games, Bobby had usually been holed up with a book.

She was quite plain back then, he remembered, but she's quite the looker now. He hoped Dan MacIsaac didn't mess about with her.

"You going down below tonight?"

"Later on, yes. I told Dan I'd look in for a bit."

"Hmm-mnh. You sure there's nothing going on there?"

"Not that again," said Roberta, a little annoyed. "Why do you bring that up again?"

"You have a funny little look on your face today."

"A funny little look? What *are* you talking about?"

"You're not in love, are you?" Rod asked.

Roberta strained to see her reflection in the glass cupboard door. She was rather flushed. "No, of course not. Don't be silly. You do talk a lot of garbage sometimes. I told you, Dan and I are just buddies."

Rod got up, walked over to the dresser and took out a large flashlight, bigger than the one he had used the night before. "Take this with you, Sis. Just in case your prowler is still around. Or I could walk you down there, if you want."

"No, that's alright. You relax and read the paper. I'll take the flashlight. Thanks."

12: She is not a whore

The Sedgemoors' living room was tastefully and expensively furnished with a mix of antique and modern furniture and fittings. The walls bore many scenes of Austria though none included any people. Some stills from *Hampton Nights* were are also dotted about the room. A huge fire was burning in the stone fireplace, although the weather was still fairly mild.

Lutzi was ensconced in a very large, high-backed arm chair staring haughtily out at the gathering night. John was behind the chesterfield, slowly pacing up and down.

"Lutzi, I do everything I can to make you comfortable. I'm sorry it isn't enough."

"Pfff! In this place? Impossible! You brought me to this place to make me unhappy."

"No, I brought you here because you said you wanted to live in a place which was very quiet. Because of your nervous condition."

"How can I remember? You are making it all up. All you ever do is aggravate my condition. I am a sick woman."

"Look, Lutzi, I know we both made a mistake, but surely to God we should try to make the best of things. You don't want me to leave, do you?"

"Ah-ha!" Lutzi shrieked. "No doubt that is what *you* want. To run away and desert me. In my condition."

"So if you don't want me to leave, let's make the effort to get along."

"You will not get the money," she said triumphantly. "I have seen to that!"

"To hell with the money," John yelled. "I don't want the stupid money. That is, if it really exists!"

"Ooh yes, the money is there." Lutzi nodded vigorously. "But not for rubbish, *und* you are rubbish. You will not touch my money. It will go to my nieces. They are of good family and breeding."

"Yes, I know that," said John wearily. "There's no point in talking to you at all, is there? You never listen to a word. Not a word."

He sat down in the opposite chair and leaned forward. "All I am saying is I try to be kind to you. The least you could do is to try to be civil to the people we meet."

"They are peasants!"

"Peasants, I see," John despaired and walked over to the fireplace. He stood for some minutes, staring into the flames.

When he turned back to her, his face had darkened. "All right. Be rude and insulting to the neighbours. Be as mean and as nasty as you like to me. But hear this, you rancorous old sow, don't you ever again fail to give me a message from the fire department! Do you hear me?" His voice has risen to an intense pitch. "I should have been at that fire. They depend on me!"

"You were too busy. You were outside with your stupid rabbits and your little whore. Imagine a grown man and his whore playing with rabbits!"

"She is not a whore!" John shouted. "She is not my anything. I only just met the woman. And that is no excuse! People's lives could have been at stake. You should have given me the message. Are you listening to me?!"

"Pfff! What do I want with stupid messages?" said Lutzi with a shrug. "Let them all burn. What do I care?"

13: Guilty conscience

The road to Dan's place was extremely dark, and only a subdued patch of the deepest indigo could be seen above the crest of the hill. Roberta's powerful flashlight pierced the blackness, stabbing this way and that, as she walked down the hill. She hummed as she went, sweeping the light from side to side, along the tree trunks which lined the banks.

As she turned into towards Dan's cabin, she heard him shouting from the jetty, "Bobby! Down here!"

Onto the planking, Dan had moved big wooden deck chairs and a small table bearing an ashtray, glasses and a bottle of Scotch. Nearby, Dan's boat was rocking gently, its rigging creaking with the motion.

Tonight, Dan wore a chunky sweater and jeans. She sat down beside him and they both gazed across the dark waters.

"Say, you haven't seen my lighter, have you?" Dan inquired.

"Your lighter? Why would I? You know I don't smoke any longer."

"It's the heavy silver one the guys gave me when I left the force."

"No. Why, you lost it?"

"Yeah, I haven't seen it in a few days. It's probably around here somewhere."

Dan stared out over the lake. Roberta sipped her Scotch, listening to the waves lapping against the jetty. From not far away, an owl hooted eerily.

Dan is not his usual easy-going self tonight, Roberta thought. He had been a little terse when they met and had almost interrogated her about the lighter. She wondered what was on his mind. Her questions were soon answered.

"So! You had a whale of a time basking in the reflected glory of our faded film star," said Dan with more than an edge of bitterness.

"What's that supposed to mean?"

"You were 'John this', 'John that' and 'John the other' earlier on when I saw you."

"Dan, that's complete nonsense!"

"Is it?"

"Anyone would think you were jealous," Roberta said with a laugh.

"Of course I am," said Dan seriously. "You know that, Bobby. You've always known that."

Roberta stared at him, thinking the suggestion ridiculous.

But she *had* known. Of course, she had known. She had known for years that Dan was more than fond of her. And she had known that she was playing with fire. Not that she was leading him on, exactly, but she had to acknowledge that neither was she actively discouraging him.

She searched her conscience, and admitted that she had enjoyed knowing there was always someone to whom she could run whenever she wanted. It suited her purposes, and her ego, to have someone who wanted her but to whom she was somewhat indifferent.

When she saw that his gaze did not leave her own, she quickly changed position in her chair, and looked away. Feeling more than a little guilty, she desperately needed to change the subject. "So, apart from that fire, did you have an exciting day?"

Dan looked at her for another second, then realized that if there ever had been a moment, it had gone. "No, not much going on," he said, trying not to sound sullen. "Skit was in for breakfast, then I took the boat out for an hour or so."

"It's good of you to feed him from time to time, although I hear Lolly takes good care of him up above."

"He drops by sometimes in the early morning when he's been poaching. Often gives me a hare he's caught. Sometimes a salmon or a lobster."

"That's nice of him. He has a sister somewhere around here, I think," Roberta said.

"Yeah, down near North Cove. Sometimes he spends the night with her and calls in on me on his way back to the farm."

"Poor Skit. I feel sorry for him."

"You shouldn't be so condescending, Bobby. In his own way he's probably a lot happier than we are."

Embarrassed again, Roberta was anxious to be gone. So she finished her drink and said her goodbyes. A loon call echoed across the lake.

~

As Roberta climbed the hill, she was still smarting. She understood Dan's attitude, but it did not make it any easier to deal with the consequences.

Her flashlight cast momentary yellow-white pools on the trees and shrubs, causing their shadows to move weirdly. About forty metres from the Gillis house, her beam caught a murky figure standing on a bank under a tree on the high side of the road and, when Roberta gasped, the figure moved, its feet crackling on twigs and leaves.

Thinking she was being chased, Roberta dashed madly towards the house, but just before she reached the driveway, she dropped to one knee, twisted around, and swung the flashlight over the road behind her.

There was nothing to see, but she could hear footsteps running away down the hill.

Breathing a heavy sigh of relief, she let herself in through the front door.

Rod was sitting on the couch, watching the *Late News*. A steaming cup of cocoa sat on a small table.

"I just saw him again," she said hotly as she entered.

"Who?"

"The watcher. For God's sake, who do you think I was talking about?"

"Oh, him. Again. Jesus. Did you get a good look at him?"

"No. I shouted at him and he ran away down the hill."

"Sounds to me like he's more scared of you than you are of him," said Rod.

"I wouldn't go that far. I'm plenty scared, I don't mind telling you!"

"Well, it seems the flashlight spooked him. Make sure you take it with you every time you go to see lover boy from now on."

"Will you knock that off? Besides I may not be going down there so often in the future."

"Something happen?" asked her brother.

"Yes and no," she said. "Sort of a combination of things. We have had something of a disagreement."

"I won't pry. It's your private business." said Rod, glad to learn there was no imminent romantic alliance between Dan MacIsaac and his sister. "I'm sure you have your reasons for keeping it to yourself."

Roberta poured a mug of cocoa for herself and they sat and sipped until the *News* was over. She hesitated, trying to find a way to broach the subject without it leading to a cross examination or a whole new series of innuendos. Finding none, she plunged straight in.

"Roddie, can you take care of the kids on Saturday afternoon? I'm going into the woods with John."

"What?" Rod sat bolt upright.

"That didn't come out right," said Roberta "I'm going mushrooming with John."

"'Mushrooming with John,'" Rod mimicked. "We are associating with high society these days."

"It isn't a problem, is it?"

"I guess not. I guess I can look after my own kids once in a while. While my sister goes 'mushrooming with John'."

"Thanks. And if you stop being an asshole, I may bring you some home for your breakfast."

14: Along a new road

It was quiet and still in the deep woods surrounding Marble Mountain. A lushness of growth was everywhere, especially on the ground, which was deeply carpeted with soft, springy, dark green moss. Just in the last few days, autumn had put forth some encroaching fingers, and at least a quarter of the hardwood leaves had turned yellow, and some were russet and gold.

Here and there, their brilliance stabbing through the verdant cover, the occasional maple leaves shone a bright, almost fluorescent salmon pink. Few birds were encountered here, but squirrels darted from tree to tree. In amongst the pillowy clumps of moss, a profusion of fungi nestled and glistened.

Large, flat baskets on their arms and knives in hands, Roberta and John slowly, carefully, picked their way along a barely-visible, overgrown trail. Seeing a cluster of bright yellow fungi, he quickly stooped to harvest them.

"Oooh," Roberta said. "They're very pretty. Are they okay?"

"Yes, these are one of the best. This is the Chanterelle. *Cantharellus cibarius*. It's a bit late in the year to be finding them. They're at the prime in August, so we probably won't find many of them today."

"I thought the brightly-coloured ones were toadstools."

"Technically, there's no such thing as a toadstool —or mushroom, for that matter. They are all fungi. Unless you can identify them, there is no way to tell a poisonous fungus from an edible one."

Roberta spied a tall, beautiful, shimmering white mushroom and reached out for it.

"Don't touch that, Bobby!" John said very quickly.

"Why?" asked Roberta, withdrawing her hand.

"That's *Amanita virosa*. It's known as the Destroying Angel."

"Ugh." Roberta shuddered. "It looks so lovely too. How poisonous is it?"

"Deadly."

"What would happen to me if I ate the whole thing?"

"It varies from person to person, but likely you'd start vomiting before nightfall, then you'd become jaundiced when your liver packed in, then after a few convulsions you'd go into a coma and be dead within forty-eight hours. That is, if you didn't get the right treatment in time. If you did there'd be chance you could make a full recovery in about two weeks."

"What kind of treatment?"

"Well, they'd have to wash you out to start with to get everything out of your stomach. Make you throw up. Then they'd pump activated charcoal through your nose for about twenty-four hours, cram a gallon of saline into your veins, and probably put you on dialysis to get the toxins out of your blood."

"Yuck. It looked so beautiful at first. Now it's giving me the creeps."

John laughed as they moved along the trail, which was now petering out. The branches were lower and they had to duck to get through.

"Now this is an interesting fungus," John said, picking up a pale brown mushroom and turning it over. "Look underneath. You see those little white teeth."

"Ooh yes. They're like tiny spines. Can you eat this one?"

"Yes, it's delicious. It's called the Hedgehog Mushroom, and you can see why. *Dentinum repandum.*"

They went further in, the trees growing closer together, and the moss becoming more bouncy, thicker, and more lush. It was heavy going now, and they had to watch their footing and duck under low-hanging branches.

"What's this one?" Roberta asked, pointing to a stocky mushroom with a whitish stalk and a rich, rusty, rounded cap.

"Aha!" John lit up. "Jackpot! That's the best of the lot. *Boletus Edulis*. The Italians call it the *Porcini* or little pig, the English call it the 'Penny Bun'. Usually we only find these in abundance when we get a very wet summer, but they're so meaty one of these is worth three of any other species."

"He's a handsome fellow, all right. I hope we find some more of those."

"We might. We might get lucky."

Deeper in the woods the sun's rays were now slanted at a shallower angle as they penetrated the forest cover like shafts of light through a cathedral window. Their baskets were filling up as they ambled along laughing and chatting like people who had known each other for a long time.

John led her to an open glade where there was a fiercely-running woodland stream, more like a small river, into which a foaming waterfall cascaded from the bedrock, the sound of the falls almost drowning out their voices. He placed his basket on the ground, arranged himself on a large, fallen tree trunk and took out a pouch of tobacco.

"Time for a rest. You don't mind if I have a pipe, do

you?"

"No, not at all. I like the smell of a pipe, especially in the open air."

Roberta found herself a hollow in the moss and made herself comfortable as John filled his briar and lit up.

"Lutzi won't let me smoke my pipe at home, not even in the garden. So the only chance I get is when I'm in the woods. It's great for keeping the bugs away. Lutzi says I have filthy habits. She says I'm rubbish."

As she studied the waterfall, Roberta wondered if she would be out line to say what was on her mind. Normally, she wouldn't dare, but she felt so comfortable with John, as if she known him much longer than a few days.

Finally, she said, "John, can I ask you a personal question?"

"Usually, I'm a very private person, Bobby, but with you I feel…I don't really know…I have known you forever. If there's anything you want to know, go ahead. I'll do my best to answer truthfully."

She looked at him for a moment, quietly amazed that they both felt as if they shared a long familiarity. "When Lutzi puts you down, you seem to let it roll right off you. But do you really mind it?"

"Yes, I do," said John with great feeling, "I mind it

terribly. In fact, I hate it!"

"Why did you marry her?"

"Ah, why indeed? That's a question I've asked myself a thousand times. I'm afraid the answer isn't very noble. You won't think well of me if I tell you."

"Try me,"

"The truth is, I think, that I married her for money —or what I thought was money. My career was in a tailspin and I didn't know what I was going to do with my life when along came Lutzi. She looked a lot better in those days and she was certainly—what shall I say?—more personable. I guess her friends had exaggerated, telling her I was a big movie star. She was flattered she could attract a so-called celebrity who also happened to be a younger man. And I went with it. Look, Bobby, I am not proud of it. In fact, I'm ashamed. Not a day goes by without accusing myself of having committed a terrible deed."

"It's understandable. You wouldn't be the first to have gone that route."

"I guess not, but it doesn't make it any more palatable, or easier to bear."

"Well," said Roberta, very much with mixed feelings, "It looks like you've paid for your mistake."

"Oh yes! I have paid. And I'm still paying. Every single day."

"Why don't you leave her?"

"I think she would be lost without me. Who else would put up with her preposterous, outrageous behaviour and her maniacal hypochondria? She couldn't survive unless she had someone to badger and berate."

"I don't know what to say," Roberta said. "I'm not sure who to feel more sorry for, you or her."

"I guess we both deserve to be shackled together for eternity," said John so sadly, that it brought a tear to Roberta's eye.

John made an indentation in the ground with his heel, tapped out his pipe ashes into it, then covered them over and pressed the earth down. He looked at her tenderly and smiled.

Roberta suddenly felt something warm inside her, a feeling she had known only once before, many years ago. The conflicted emotions she felt when he had described his disreputable liaison with Lutzi had vanished. His absolute honesty and abject misery seized her with equal measures of admiration and pity. She felt she was striking out along a new road and that, even had she wanted to, it was one from which there would be no turning back.

"Time to be getting back," he said, reaching out and touching her arm.

They stood up, brushed themselves down and gathered up their baskets.

"We've got a pretty good haul here," he said.

"Yes. I can't wait to get back and taste these mushrooms. They all look delicious."

They stood in silence, looking at the falls for a few minutes, then simultaneously turned to face each other, speaking at the same time.

"I've had a wonderful day," Roberta said so quietly she could barely be heard over the falls.

"Yes, so have I." John shifted his basket to the other arm.

Another silence overtook them as they watched the relentless water, interminably pouring from the source above, forming a multitude of rivulets until they merged into one force crashing down on the rocks below, spraying the surrounding ferns.

"Do you think…"John broke off.

"Think what?"

"Do you think we should do this again?"

"I've been thinking about that," Roberta said, "It could be…er… unpredictable."

"Yes, I know. It could be very unpredictable. Maybe dangerous."

"I'll risk it if you will." Roberta had not intended to say that, but found herself blurting it out anyway.

"Me too," said John decisively, striding away.

15: I was only passing

During the next few days, the heavens opened. It was not a violent, windswept, blustery kind of rain, but a steady, never-ending, depressing, remorseless downpour with no redeeming feature. Except that is, if it ever stopped, there would be an enormous bounty of mushrooms for her and John.

But until it did stop, there would be no chance of her seeing him. He had no legitimate reason to visit the Gillis place, and she certainly has no valid excuse to visit him at 'Castle Lutzi', as he had come to call their house.

Roberta remembered a rhyme from her childhood:

> *Rain, rain, go away*
> *Come again some other day*
> *We want to go outside and play*
> *Come again some other day*
> *Rain, rain, go away*

Come again some other day
We want to go outside and play
Come again some other day
Rain, rain, go away
Come again some other day
We want to go outside and play
Come again some other day

Having seen the children off to school and taken care of her mother, Roberta just moped about the place, spending most of the time just gazing out of the windows into the continuous rain. Not that there was much to see, visibility being almost zero and only the nearest trees were within the field of vision.

Not being able to get even a glimpse of the Lakes was especially dispiriting, and she realized how much she missed that pleasure. There was something uplifting, almost spiritual, in regularly being able to look across an expanse of water and seeing life on the other side. She also became aware of how much she took for granted the constant presence, under normal conditions, of a wide variety of birds: crows, gulls, terns, eagles, ducks, geese, grackles, sparrows, even puffins and the occasional gannet.

After a nominal amount of housework, there was nothing to do but think.

Think. She couldn't stop thinking about John. She

had replayed in her mind their day in the woods, over and over until it almost made her ill. She wondered what their next meeting would be like.

Would something dramatic happen, or would they both be too scared and carry on as though everything was normal?

She even wondered what their life would like together, but each time she allowed her daydreams to proceed beyond vague idyllic generalities, Lutzi's face loomed before her, demanding: *What are you? Are you a whore?*

Was she? No, she definitely decided, I am not that. Not yet, anyway.

Once, she did put on rain gear and ventured down to Dan's, but she found him less than hospitable.

"Hello, Sergeant," she said, trying to sound friendly, as she stood dripping on his deck.

"Oh, it's you."

"Going to ask me in?"

"Sure, if you want."

Dan was clearly not in a good mood. She wondered if he ever would be again. Maybe this was his way of punishing her for not reciprocating his feelings.

"I won't disturb you if you're busy." She felt obliged to offer him a way out.

He took it. "The place is at sixes and sevens right

now," he mumbled. "I was giving it a good clean out."

"Okay. No problem," Roberta did her best to sound cheerful. "I was only passing."

"Yeah, okay. See you, Bobby."

"See you, Dan," she said, turning back into the downpour.

He had left her standing in the wet the whole time, she reflected indignantly. He offered her no coffee, and certainly no Scotch. It seemed as if he were making a major effort to be even civil.

Well, if that's how he wants to play it, that's fine with me, she told herself.

But later, on the hill, soaking wet, she felt inexpressibly sad, almost deprived. She hoped she had not lost forever a certain something which was, after all, very important to her.

The older children found her unusually distant, hard to engage, but, sensing she was not herself, wisely gave her space. But Angie followed her around, clinging to her legs, pulling at her clothing, seeking the attention Roberta was unable to give in full.

Rod, whose antennae were surprisingly well-developed, knew there was something afoot, something which was deeply affecting his sister. He suspected that it was "man trouble", but wrongly thought it had everything to do with Dan MacIsaac.

He was sufficiently worried that one night he decided to tackle her head on, so after the children had gone to bed, he broached the matter. "What's on your mind, Bobby?"

"Hmm?"

"I said, what's on your mind?"

"Why should anything be on my mind?"

"Come on, Sis, I've known you for forty years. I know when something is up."

"It's private," she said. "And anyway, it would be too difficult to explain."

"Try me."

"I'm not even sure I know what is going on, myself. It's all muddled up."

"It's a guy, isn't it?"

"Why should it be a guy?" Roberta tried to parry him.

"I'm one myself, remember, and I know what utter bastards we can be," said Rod.

"No, no. It's nothing like that. I can tell you, nobody has done anything to me along those lines. It's not what you think."

"You must be in love, then."

"Must I? Is that what you believe?"

"You're showing all the signs, Bobby. Is it Danny Fiddles?"

"What?" She was annoyed he would still think she

would be involved with Dan. "No, of course not."

"Then who? Who else do you know around here? "

She remained silent, staring at her feet. Suddenly, Rod said, "Oh my God! It's him! It's that Sedgemoor guy! Holy crap!"

"Look Rod," Roberta was serious. "I don't know what's going on. There could be something. That's all."

"But you want it to be something?"

She was picking at a thread in her sweater. She said nothing.

"Don't you?" Rod persisted.

"Oh, alright, yes." Roberta sounded tormented, almost in anguish. "But please leave me alone now. Please. I'll let you know if anything develops."

"Okay, Sis." His words were kind, but cautionary. "I sure hope you know what you you're doing."

16: Making a mistake?

At long last, the rain stopped and the sun came streaming through the early morning windows.

Roberta saw the sunlight out of one eye, leaped out of bed and ripped the curtains open. Her heart soared.

She ran out onto the landing and shouted, "Rise and shine, my angels! It's a beautiful day!"

Grabbing her robe, she raced downstairs, singing,

> *Good morning to you! Good morning to you!*
> *We're all in our places With sun-shiny faces;*
> *Oh this is the way To start a new day!*
> *Good morning to you! Good morning to you!*
> *Whatever the weather, We'll make it together,*
> *In work and in play, A beautiful day!*
> *Good Morning to you.*
> *Good morning to you.*
> *Good morning dear children*
> *Good morning to all.*

The children emerged from their rooms, staring at each other.

"What's up with her?" asked Brad.

"I don't know," said Angie sweetly, "but I'm so glad Aunty Bob is happy again."

Roberta continued to sing while she fed the children their breakfast. They in turn, rolled their eyes and giggled, but she didn't mind.

It was a fantastic day, indeed, and when she strained through the kitchen window to see high in the sky, she could not discern a single cloud. However, she immediately noticed that during the past few days the leaves had undergone a radical chance. Now, except for the conifers, there was almost no green to be seen, but the yellow was deeper, brighter and there was much more orange in the foliage.

It would be the perfect day for mushrooming, and maybe for an exciting adventure of the heart.

She couldn't call John because she knew Lutzi might answer, but she was sure John would contrive to contact her so they could go into the woods again. She bustled the older children off to school, and waited impatiently for Mrs. MacLeod to come for Angie.

While they were waiting on the stoop the phone rang.

"I'll have to answer that Angie," said Roberta. "If

Mrs. MacLeod comes while I'm on the phone, you go on. I'll see you tonight."

She raced through to the kitchen, her heart in her mouth. "Hello. Gillis residence."

"Mrs. Gillis?" It was not John, but an unknown female voice.

"Mrs. Gillis died a few weeks ago, but I am Mr. Gillis' sister."

"Ah, I understand," said the woman, "This is Agnes Matheson from Social Services. You are the one I want to talk to. I think we have a place for your mother."

"Oh, good. When do you think she could move in?"

"Well, I need you to come to Port Hawkesbury. We will go over the paper work and then go to see the facility. I need to know you're happy with what we provide. If you are, it would take some days after that."

"Of course," said Roberta. "When do you want to see me?"

"Later today would be best. Can you get here before lunch time?"

"Yes, I think so. Do you think it will take long to sort out?" Roberta said, rather too quickly.

"Well, we want to be thorough," said the voice, clearly put out. "The paperwork is a bit involved. It takes as long as it takes."

"Yes, of course. I'm sorry. I'll be there."

"Fine. I'll see you later," said Mrs. Matheson, ringing off.

Damn!

Of course, she was glad that her mother's situation had been resolved. Clearly, Rod could not continue to work as well as cope with their mother once Roberta was gone, but it meant another day apart from John and tomorrow it might be raining again.

The phone rang again and she snatched it up. "Yes," she said breathlessly.

"It's me. Lutzi's out in the yard. Meet you at the bridge in an hour."

"Oh John," she almost wailed, "I can't. I have to go to the Strait to see about a nursing home for my mother."

"Curses!" said John. "Okay. Tomorrow. Same time, same place?"

"I'll be there!"

"Great! Got to go. Lutzi's coming back in."

The line clicked and went dead.

Her heart was literally pounding. And this effect was produced by merely talking to him on the phone. How, she wondered, would her heart react when finally they met the next day.

Tomorrow! That made the waiting all right. That made the chore of going to the Strait worthwhile.

She fleetingly remembered the closing passage of James Joyce's *Ulysses*, where Molly Bloom surrenders to her lover with the words: *I drew him down to me so he could feel my breasts all perfume yes and his heart was going like mad and yes I said yes I will Yes.*

That is exactly how she felt. If John were to ask her to go with him, she would say yes, yes, yes.

~

As Roberta was changing into more business-like clothes and shoes, her euphoric mood changed. She now started to feel a little soiled, and more than a trifle guilty. Here they were skulking around like teenagers breaking curfew, no, more like criminals.

Adultery! If this ended where she thought it was heading, they would have committed adultery. In that event, she wondered if just John would be an adulterer or would she also be one?

Exhilarated on the one hand, troubled on the other, she drove down through West Bay to Cleveland, and onto Highway Four. She got stuck behind a pulp truck for some time, but was in Port Hawkesbury within the hour. She found the Social Services building, parked and went in to see Mrs. Matheson.

The nursing home seemed very comfortable and the staff were friendly and helpful, but Mrs. Matheson was a different matter. Describing herself as a Care Coordinator, she was methodical to a tedious degree, requiring a letter from Mrs. Gillis' doctor, her medical history and consent for a physical examination, information about her income and pension details, and a host of forms to be filled out.

Roberta would not have minded if Mrs. Matheson had not treated her like a child, repeating each question several times.

Eventually, though, it was all done, except for getting Rod's signature on some documents, but it was after three o'clock when she got out of there. There was no chance of her reinstating the rendezvous with John today.

~

Later that night, after the children had gone to bed. Roberta and Rod were hanging over the rail of the back deck. It was another spectacularly starry night, which Roberta thought bode well for her assignation with John the next day

"I'm glad that's settled," said Rod. "Poor old Ma. When can they move her in?"

"The end of next week, I think. We'll get the final details after you drop off those forms you signed. You will do that?"

"Yeah. I'll do it tomorrow after work."

"Will the office still be open?"

"Ah. I can sneak out in my lunch break and get them up there."

"I'll take her down next week," said Roberta. "Then I think I'll head on to Antigonish to do some shopping. Anything you want while I'm there?"

"You can get me that drill bit I've been wanting. I tried Canadian Tire at the Strait, but they didn't have it."

"Sure. No problem."

Rod looked up at the stars, sighed and rubbed his face with his hand. Roberta guessed what was coming.

"On this other thing. You know what you were saying?"

"What was I saying?"

"About John Sedgemoor."

"What about him?"

"I don't really know what to tell you, Bobby. I mean, you're a big girl now, so I guess you ought to know what you're doing."

"I'm not entirely sure I do," said Roberta.

"Well, you'd better find out before somebody gets hurt."

"I'll try."

"One other thing."

"What?"

"Whatever happens, whatever you decide, you know I'll always have your back, Sis."

"Thanks, big brother. That means a lot."

~

The next day fulfilled all her expectations. If anything, it was even more glorious than the day before, and now there was gold all over the hills, with brilliant red patches shining through.

Roberta packed the children off to school, then tiptoed (she didn't know why) to the end of the hallway to her mother's room, knocked timidly, then crept in.

As every day, she brushed Mrs. Gillis' long white hair in a rhythmic motion.

"So that's the whole story, Ma. What do you think?"

Gazing out of the window, the old lady showed no sign of having heard and still less of comprehending.

Roberta continued to brush. "Do you think I'm making a mistake, Ma?"

The silence was broken only by the creaking of the old rocking chair.

"Am I really doing something wrong?"

Her mother moved her head ever so slightly.

Roberta quickly leaned over her, looking intently for some sign, but there was no expression to be seen. "Will you miss us, I wonder, in the new place?"

She stared at her for a second, then said, "No, of course you won't."

Then she added, "But I think we might miss you."

Roberta sang softly to her.

> *Down in the valley,*
> *The valley so low,*
> *Hang your head over,*
> *And hear the winds blow.*
> *Roses love sunshine,*
> *Violets love dew*
> *Angels in heaven*
> *Know I love you.*

The old lady continued to rock gently as Roberta quietly left the room.

17: You saved my life!

Roberta arrived at the bridge quite a bit earlier than the appointed time, so she hoisted herself up onto its rail, and kicked her heels against the rail supports.

She noticed that swallows, their bright-blue backs flashing in the sunlight, were swooping over the brook where a myriad of tiny insects were swarming. They were not common visitors in these parts, staying mostly in the lowland areas of Eastern Cape Breton, but it was thrilling to see them as they effortlessly swooped, ducked and dived about.

She heard the sound of a vehicle and, feeling as if her heart had almost stopped, she slid down from the rail and waited expectantly. But it was Norman MacKenzie, the storekeeper, in his van, to whom she grinned and waved. He returned the gesture and quickly disappeared.

Roberta eagerly consulted her watch. It was now past time. Maybe he isn't coming. Maybe Lutzi had caught him trying to sneak away. Maybe she would have to wait another day before she saw him.

Then, suddenly, there he was, handsome and smiling behind the wheel of his BMW station wagon. How wonderful she felt. How marvellous it was to be alive, but how nerve-racking to be embarking on a dangerous adventure.

She ran to the vehicle, jumped in and, without hesitation, snuggled as close to him as she could get.

"I have missed you so much," John said quite simply.

"Me too," Roberta said, "I mean I've missed you, not that I've missed me!"

They laughed freely.

"Where are we going?"

"Somewhere special," said John, "somewhere where there will be more mushrooms and even more privacy."

"Oooh." Roberta felt a thrill running through her. "Let's go!"

They took off, their spirits and expectations high, but no sooner had they gone a little more than a kilometre when they saw smoke billowing from the MacDonald farm.

John immediately pulled the wagon to the side of the road, stopped and rushed around to the rear door.

"Move over," John said to Roberta "You drive while

I change into my fire-fighting outfit."

He dragged his helmet, boots and protective clothing from the back, then clambered into the passenger seat. While Roberta pulled the car back onto the road, John struggled to get into his gear.

When they screeched into the MacDonald's yard, Lolly, Randy and Lavender were helplessly watching the barn blaze away. Swaying from side to side, Skit stood mesmerized by the flames which were reflected on his weirdly-contorted face.

Soon other vehicles, including the local fire truck, came lumbering up the track. Roberta quickly pulled the car to one side of the yard to clear a path for them, then she and John, now fully equipped, scrambled out to face the chaotic scene. A number of neighbours, on foot, swarmed in behind them.

In no time, the firemen had unloaded their equipment and started to pump their hoses at the fire. The Fire Chief, Willy MacKinnon, barked orders left and right and his men swiftly carried them out. John and Roberta ran over to where the MacDonalds were standing.

"My God, Lolly. What happened?" asked Roberta.

"No idea, Bobby. I just looked out the kitchen window and there she was, a'goin' up in smoke."

"Are you all okay?" Asked John.

"Yeah, we're in one piece, just about," said Randy.

"Is there anything of value in the barn?"

"No dear," said Lolly "not really. The hay is the only thing worth having and there wasn't much of that yet. We ain't taken it in yet this year."

Suddenly, Lavender screamed at the top of her voice.

Shocked and astonished they all turned to her. "What is it, Lavvy?" Roberta said.

"Grampy Linus!"

Lolly and Randy spoke at the same time, their words tumbling out.

"Oh my God, I forgot all about Linus," said Randy.

"He's still in there!" Lolly cried.

"Where? The barn?" John was stern and alert.

"No, the shed that's tacked on to the back," Randy said.

"Show me!" John demanded curtly. "Take me there now!"

As Randy, Roberta and John raced around the corner of the barn, heading for Linus's hut, a blazing timber pulled loose from the roof and crashed onto the pile of tires and boxes, which instantly burst into flames.

"The hut looks okay," shouted Randy above the roar, "but the door is on the other side of them tires. It's the only way in."

"You'll never be able to get through those flames!"

Roberta cried. "Poor old Linus."

But, without a moment's hesitation, John put his head down and charged through the inferno, smashing to the left and right with his axe, dislodging some blazing tires which then crazily rolled into the yard.

Huge clouds of thick, black, foul-smelling smoke enveloped a spluttering and coughing Roberta and Randy. They staggered about, trying to get their bearings, then retreated some metres and stood staring hypnotically into the fire.

Several minutes passed, during which Roberta suffered a thousand agonies, believing she would never see John again. Then, as the wind changed the direction of the smoke, they saw John lurching towards them carrying Linus in his arms.

"Jesus, that was a close shave," said Linus. "What kept you, boy? You sure took your time. Another minute and I'd have been friggin' toast!"

John passed Linus to Randy, who immediately headed off towards the house, barely able to keep his footing among the debris.

Roberta ran to John wrapping her arms around him. "Dear God, I thought I'd lost you." Tears were running down her cheeks. "Are you alright? Are you hurt anywhere? John, speak to me."

"I'm fine," said John, sounding far from fine, coughing loudly and clinging to her for support. "I'll be okay."

John was streaked with soot and his eyes were raw red. He looked at Roberta and saw the depth of her concern and relief in her face. Both realizing this was a point of no return, they gazed transfixed at each other as the dancing flames were reflected in their eyes.

Two firemen came up, peeled John away from her and, one on each side, guided him to the house.

At a distance Dan MacIsaac, watched this scene unfold, then, after a few seconds, stepped into Roberta's path. "Hey, Bobby. Surprised to see you here. What a terrible mess."

"Oh! Hi, Dan. Yes, terrible. Thank God nobody was hurt."

"Well, I better get back to work. There's still some burning and we've got an awful lot of clearing out to do."

"Okay."

"Come down tomorrow," said Dan as he turned away. "we'll go out in the boat and get some fish."

"Yes, okay." She didn't refuse because she did not have the strength to argue.

~

The inside of the MacDonald house was like something out of a Bruegel painting. The kitchen was packed to the rafters with firefighters, neighbours, dogs, cats, puppies and kittens.

Lolly, her face streaming with perspiration, dashed around making tea, cutting bread for sandwiches, handing out cake and trying to bring some kind of order to the chaos.

Seated in a prominent position on the edge of the table, Linus held forth on his recent scrape with death. Randy had a female neighbour pinned against the fridge, his face so close he was almost licking her. She, in turn, showed every sign of succumbing to his advances. Lavender was seen slinking away with a strapping young firefighter to places unknown. A much blackened and dishevelled John, the centre of attention, was gratefully drinking a beer and receiving words of praise and congratulation from every quarter.

Every so often Linus waved across the room in his direction and shouted, "There's the man who saved my life!"

Roberta, being elbowed and jostled by well-wishers, tried to stay as close as she could to John, all the while carefully watching him for signs of injury or fatigue. From a corner, Dan glumly observed the festivities.

When she saw that everyone had received food

and drink, Lolly tried to give a little speech of thanks, but was drowned out by the general hubbub, so with a laugh she gave up the effort and flopped down into a big chair. Immediately two cats leapt up on to her lap.

"I'm bushed," said John, rising from his chair. "I hope nobody minds if I push off."

"You saved my life!" cried Linus.

"I was happy to be of service, Linus. I hope I don't have to do it again in a while."

Everybody laughed and, with much back-slapping and friendly banter, John fought his way through the throng. Roberta followed at a discreet distance.

Outside, it was dark now, but with a good, bright moon up above. Covered with still slightly smoking debris, the yard glistened from the gallons of water which been pumped earlier.

Roberta caught up with John and slipped her arm through his. He gave her a smile of ineffable fondness.

Behind them, the back door opened with a burst of light, and revealed that Dan was watching them walk away.

After they had negotiated their way through more wreckage and hoses, John and Roberta noticed a firefighter's clothing on the ground by the corner of the cowshed. They exchanged puzzled glances, then peered around the doorway.

There against the wall a fireman, naked from the waist down, was copulating with an enthusiastic Lavender. Her smiling face peeped over the fireman's shoulder and gave them a broad wink.

"I have to say, that looked like fun," said John as they went over to his car.

"Yes, it did," said Roberta with a hearty laugh, then added, "It's been a long time."

"You too?" He reached out and pulled her towards him. "Sadly, this is all you're going to get tonight."

He kissed her very gently. She did not mind the soot and grime on his face, or the beer on his breath, or the soaked clothing pressing against her, or the smell of smoke and burning tires.

"John, what are we going to do?"

"I don't know, Bobby. We'll think of something."

He drove her to the Gillis house, and before she got out they kissed again.

"I'll be in touch," he said, then drove off into the night.

18: A completely disinterested party

Rod was waiting at the door, clearly anxious. Naturally, word of the MacDonalds' fire had quickly spread around the neighbourhood, but he had not dreamed his sister would have been at the site, so he asked her how she came to be there. When she explained the circumstances, he frowned.

"So you're obviously one step closer," said Rod, "Are you committed yet?"

"I'm afraid I am, Rod. Very committed."

"Okay. Not sure how this is going to play out. It'll be a hell of a mess, that's for sure, but I hope you'll be happy."

"Thanks, brother, so do I."

"Well, I guess that's enough excitement for one day. We'd better get to bed. Some of us actually have to work."

The next day, after she had seen the children off to school, she remembered her promise to go fishing with Dan. She did not at all feel like going. She was afraid he might be churlish and argue with her about John. It gave her a gnawing feeling in the pit of her stomach. She knew that if, even now, John got in touch, she would have reneged on the appointment in a trice, but he did not call.

So she got her gear together and headed off down the hill.

"Morning. Sergeant," she greeted him.

"Oh hi, Bobby."

"So, we're going fishing?"

"Sure. I've got some coffee and sandwiches we can have when we're out there."

Dan seemed unusually taciturn as he loaded the boat and pushed off from the jetty. They sat in silence as they headed out into the lakes, a brisk wind whipping at their sail. They continued until the little sailing boat was far out beyond West Bay.

One glance across the shining blue waters to the landscape beyond was enough to reveal that autumn was gaining ground rapidly. Ochre and orange were now the predominant colours of the hardwoods, with pinks and reds more frequent than heretofore. Leaves drifted in the water, and here and there trees thrust their half-naked branches into the air. There were very few bugs now, and geese were beginning to gather to begin their journey to gentler climes.

The sky was still blue, but the deepness had gone. The clouds were a little lower and the breezes now had a chilly edge.

Dan took in the sail, dropped anchor, and set up his fishing rod. He laid out the contents of a small picnic basket on the deck, handed Roberta a sandwich and then unscrewed a thermos flask. He passed her a coffee in a plastic cup.

"Bobby, you know you're making a mistake, don't

you?"

Roberta stiffened. She had been expecting a lecture. Now here it was. She took a mouthful of sandwich in order to prolong her silence.

"You know what I'm talking about. You should put a stop to it while you still can."

Roberta glared at him, still saying nothing.

"Don't pretend, Bobby," Dan persisted. "You know I'm talking about you and Sedgemoor. A married man."

"Have you been spying on me?"

"No, of course not. I just couldn't help noticing. It's not like you're going to much trouble to hide it. And this is a small community."

"And I guess you're a completely disinterested party," Roberta said savagely. "No axe to grind. Nothing like that!"

"I didn't say that," said Dan a little hurt. "I guess you know how I feel about you, Bobby. The way I've always felt about you. Going back years."

"Yes, I guess so. I guess I might have thought something of the sort."

"But I'd still give you the same advice even if things were different."

"Your advice is duly noted, Sergeant."

They hung about, largely in silence except for the water lapping against the boat, for another hour. Dan caught nothing so gave up, reeled in and stowed his gear, weighed anchor and headed for shore.

As they made fast the boat, Dan said, "Are we still friends, Bobby? I'd hate us not to be friends."

"Yep. If you want. Friends."

"Shake on it, Sergeant?"

"Okay, Sergeant," said Bobby, offering her hand.

19: There was that word again

The Community Recreation Centre Hall was a long, white, wooden building situated by the side of the road and overlooking the lakes. It was surrounded by cars and trucks parked in a disorderly, unsystematic fashion. Further vehicles stretched out along the roadside for about half a mile.

People on foot were surging towards the hall as sounds of voices and music emitted from its windows. Outside was a hand-written sign:

BENEFIT SUPPER
FOR MACDONALD'S BARN
TONITE. 7.00

Inside, long tables covered with paper cloths, and with rough wooden benches on either side, were crammed with local residents. Those who had come early were already starting on home-made pie, while later arrivals were still lined up waiting for turkey or stew.

A resting trio of musicians, occupying the corner of a small stage, were chatting and drinking beer from cans. The noise level of the conversations and clanging pots and pans was almost deafening.

Roberta, Rod, Bonnie, Brad and Angie sat at a table with Lolly, Randy and Lavender, while John, a committee member, was earnestly conferring with storekeeper Norman MacKenzie at the edge of the stage. Lutzi, having amazed everyone by deigning to even show up, sat imperiously by herself at the back of the room, conspicuously sneering at everything she saw.

Norman, a bustling, portly, white-haired man in his sixties, mounted the stage and called for attention. "Ladies and gentlemen and friends."

He had a rich bass voice which had been heard at many a function over many years. "Thank you all for turning out here tonight to support a worthy cause, namely to help replace Lolly MacDonald's barn, which she lost in a fire last week."

There was applause, mixed with shouts of approval.

Norman waved his hands for silence, then continued. "It is my pleasure to announce that, between the ticket sales for this supper and a number of donations, we have already raised over two thousand dollars."

There were loud cheers and foot stamping from the audience.

"Thank you, thank you. Now, since we have eleven husky men who have volunteered to work on the rebuilding, I should say we can at least make a good start on her before the snow flies."

"I hope your name is on that list, Norm," shouted a man in the audience. "You could use the exercise!"

The crowd erupted into fits of laughter and whistles.

"Yes sir," said Norman. "My name is on the list. Which is more than I can say for yours, Lauchie Murray!"

The crowed hooted and jeered the heckler, who scowled back.

"Who knows? With a bit of luck we might finish the barn before winter," said Norman to more applause. "I would be remiss in my duties if I did not thank the executive of the Recreation Association for hosting us tonight, and for the Ladies' Auxiliary for providing a beautiful supper."

This received prolonged applause and much cheering.

"Now, last but not least, I want to thank our good friend John Sedgemoor for organizing this event tonight. He's not been amongst us for very long, but he's sure turned out to be one hell of a neighbour."

"He saved my life!" Shouted Linus. "He's a hero!"

This was greeted by very loud applause and more foot stamping. Some people were banging their knives on the tables.

As this died down, Lutzi rose in her place like an avenging angel. "What do you know?" she yelled. "You know nothing! You call this man a hero. Pfff! You should know him like I do!"

"There's my biggest fan," said John, an artificial grin plastered on his face.

The crowd laughed with John, but they were clearly uneasy now, giving each other sidelong glances. From where she sat, Roberta could feel John's discomfort.

Sensing trouble, Norman bustled forward, his arms raised. "All right, now! Order, please. Moving right along, I see Bobby Gillis back there. Nice to see you home again, Bobby. She's been up in Ontario for a few years, but is back visiting her brother, Rod."

There were a few appreciative remarks from some of the men.

"Looking good, Bobby."

"Meet me outside after, Bobby."

"Now, now," said Norman, "those of you who knew Bobby in the old days know she is a fine singer, and her brother Rod told me I should get up here to give us a tune."

The crowd cheered this announcement heartily.

Roberta gasped, turned to a grinning Rod, glared at him and mouthed, "You bastard."

Reluctantly, she went forward, borrowed a guitar from one of the musicians and started to sing softly.

The audience was mesmerized by the sweetness of her voice, but before the last verse was over, Lutzi jumped up and walked to the door.

There she turned, and loudly said, "That's the hero's whore!"

Stunned, Roberta stopped singing and dissolved in embarrassment and confusion. Loud muttering and clucking swept the room.

John, his face as black as thunder, stared at Lutzi's back as she marched out of the hall.

The event descended into chaos and Norman MacKenzie was totally unable to restore order. The place erupted with chattering and the noise of people getting up from their benches and pouring out into the night.

Everyone except the musicians and the serving ladies had left the hall. The Gillis family sat at their table in stunned silence, Roberta in tears. John had gone storming after Lutzi, and Roberta could well imagine the scene that would ensue.

Brad, anxious to be gone, was fidgeting and playing with the cutlery. Bonnie seemed dazed by the unfolding of events. Angie was half asleep.

Norman MacKenzie was in the porch in earnest conversation with the priest, Father MacIntyre. Neither was making any attempt to keep his voice down.

"No Father, I did not know." Norman was insisting on his innocence in the whole debacle. "I had no idea."

"It's a bad business, no and mistake," said the priest "Bad for the parish. Bad for everyone."

"Yes, Father. I agree."

"All right, Norman. I'm away to the glebe. Not in all my years in the priesthood have I seen anything as scandalous. You had better make sure this sort of thing doesn't become a regular occurrence."

"No, no, of course not, Father."

Father MacIntyre disappeared into the night, his soutane flapping around his legs.

Hesitantly, Norman re-entered the room and came up to the Gillises. "I'm sorry about this, Rod." He shook his head. "Who would have thought something like this could happen around here?"

"What you mean is that we just say these things in private," said Rod ruefully, "but never in public."

"I'm not sure that's fair. Today was the first time I heard of it."

"In a way I guess it's my own fault," sobbed Roberta, "but she's a spiteful, hateful old cow anyway."

"There's no denying that," said Norman. Then he looked around the room. "We'd best all be out of here now so the women can clear up."

"Okay, Norm," said Rod. "We're going."

They dragged themselves to their feet and went out into the darkness. It was quite chilly, but the moon was riding high in the sky. In a state of profound gloom, they piled into Rod's Cherokee.

On the short ride home, Angie stirred. "Aunty Bob."

"Yes, sweetheart?"

"There was that word again tonight."

"What word, honey?"

"Whore. I still don't know what it means."

"Go back to sleep, Angie," said Roberta, the tears welling up again.

"Okay, Aunty Bob."

As soon as they got home, Rod chased the children off to bed with strict instructions not to discuss the day's events at home, and certainly not at school. He told them to ignore all impertinent questions from other children and all gossip they heard.

"It's all a tempest in a teapot," he told them, "but until it blows over I want you all to be very kind to Bobby. As a special favour to me."

Having obtained a solemn promise from each of them, he switched out their lights. Before he went downstairs he rummaged in a closet on the landing until he found a bottle he had been given as a present years before. He went into the living room, brandishing it to Roberta.

"A night like this one calls for something a bit special," he said, holding the bottle under a table lamp and reading off the label. "Abelour Single Malt. 18 years old. Sounds like just what we need."

"You can say that again," said Roberta. "Where did you get that? That stuff is pretty rare and very expensive."

"You know I'm not normally a Scotch drinker. I didn't buy it. Old Mr. Mac Fadgen gave it to me when I did some work on his place at Lake Ainslie a few years ago. He said he had a collection of some of the best Scotches in the world, but his doctor told him he couldn't touch it any more. Actually, he gave me two bottles but I gave the other one to a guy from Scotland I was working with at the time."

He gently poured the rich, warm, amber liquor into two glasses, and handed one to her. They sniffed it appreciatively, smelling sherry, honey, and spices in its generous heart. They sat back, put up their feet on the coffee table and drank in silence.

Finally Rod spoke. "That was some fucking shit

show, Sis, and no mistake!”

“I know. Nobody is more sorry than me.”

“No, I’m sorry you had to go through it. That vicious old bitch should be horsewhipped.”

“That was my reaction too,” said Roberta, “but you can understand where she’s coming from. She’s sick, she’s in a strange land with people she doesn’t know, and she thinks some floozy is stealing her husband. The ironic thing is what she says is not really true.”

“What does ‘not really’ mean?”

“I swear to God, the only thing that has passed between John and me is a quick kiss at the MacDonalds’ fire.”

“But...”

“But, what?”

“But you’re not going to leave it at that, are you?”

Roberta smiled affectionately at her brother, then took a large mouthful of the Abelour. “God, this is amazing stuff,” she said. “May I have some more?”

“Sure,” said Rod, getting up and pouring her another measure. “Have as much as you like.”

“Thanks for everything, Roddie,” she said, raising her glass. “Here’s to never having another evening like today’s.”

“I’ll drink to that!” said Rod with complete conviction. “When are you going to see him again?”

“Maybe tomorrow.”

"Trouble is your middle name," her brother said. He drained his glass. "I'm off to bed."

"Me, too. G'night."

20: The whole thing is made up!

The next day, after Rod had gone to work and the children had been dispatched to school, Roberta was washing dishes in the sink when there was a knock at the back door.

John poked his head around the opening. "Can I come in?"

"John!"

"Darling!"

Roberta ran to him, threw her arms around him and started to sob. "God, that was so awful yesterday. You must have been even more mortified than I was."

"I doubt that," said John. "You can't begin to imagine the things I said to her when I got home."

Roberta went over to the table to get a Kleenex from her purse. "Does she know?" she asked, dabbing her eyes. "What does she suspect? I mean, it's not even true...not...yet."

"She knows nothing. And I don't really think she

believes anything is going on. It's just her way of being bloody minded."

"What are we going to do, John?" Roberta almost wailed.

"I'll take care of it. By the time I get back, I'll have something worked out."

"Back? What do you mean? Where are you going?"

"I didn't have a chance to tell you yesterday, but I have to go to England to see my brother. It's family stuff. Some problems with our aunt's property. It's been festering for some time, now we really have to deal with it. Apparently, it's all coming to a head."

"Oh." Roberta was floored by this news. To have John taken away from her this soon was a real blow. "Where does your brother live, in London?"

"No, in Bristol. That's about a hundred miles from London. I'll have to rent a car at Heathrow."

"I can't believe this. I'll miss you terribly. How long will you be gone?"

"Just two weeks."

"Two weeks! That will seem like forever." Roberta was bereft. "When do you have to leave?"

"The day after tomorrow, I thought. I was hoping you'd drive me to Sydney. We could stay the night there and then I'll get a flight to Halifax the next day and then on to London."

"Sure, that'd be nice. Of course, I'd love to drive

you." She took in a sharp intake of breath. "And stay the night."

"I was hoping you'd say that. I thought we could take our time and drive the scenic route to Sydney through Iona."

"Lovely, but I'll have to sort something out with Rod about the kids."

"Yes, of course."

"What about Lutzi? What will she think if I drive you to Sydney?"

"To hell with Lutzi!"

"Tsk, tsk."

"Anyhow, things to do now. A lot to arrange: hotels, flights, cars. So I'll love you and leave you."

"Do you really mean that—about loving me?"

"Oh yes," said John solemnly, "very much indeed."

They embraced and kissed many times, over many minutes, before she shooed John out of the door and returned to her housework.

As she worked, Roberta sung her heart out.

Moonlight and roses
Bring wonderful memories of you
My heart reposes
In beautiful thoughts, so true
June light discloses
Love's golden dreams sparkling anew

Moonlight and roses
Bring memories of you.
June light discloses
Love's golden dreams sparkling anew
Moonlight and roses
Bring memories of you

The mood at the Sedgemoor residence was not nearly as upbeat it was at the Gillis place. An atmosphere of profound gloom enveloped the house. Try as he might, John's efforts to placate Lutzi were all in vain, and she was determined to be both victim and aggressor at the same time

"I do not even believe you have a brother," she declared. "How could someone like you have a brother?"

"Lutzi, don't be ridiculous. You know I have a brother. He was at our wedding, for God's sake!"

"How do I know he was not one of your actor friends from your television days? *Ja,* an actor! The whole thing is made up!"

"There's no point in arguing the point," said John, exasperated. "I'm going to England and that's that."

"To England! Pfff! That is what you say, but you are probably going to Hawaii, or Caribbean, or to Bora Bora with your whore."

"That's a lot of nonsense and you know it."

"No, I do not know any such thing! You will be having the time of your lives. In luxury and sinfulness."

They glared at each other for several minutes. John was anxious not to give Lutzi any further ammunition with which she could lambaste him, but the effort was in vain.

"I suppose you'll be all right here on your own while I'm gone?"

"That's right, leave me all alone, and in my condition. You should be ashamed!"

Lutzi stuck her chin in the air, then in a different vein, continued, "But don't worry about me. I will be fine. I am going to enjoy being without you. Without rubbish."

"Good, I'm glad."

"I will go on the town," she pronounced defiantly. "I will buy things. I will eat at restaurants. I will stay at hotels!"

"You won't find too much in Antigonish which is up to your standards," John observed. "Besides, how will you get there?"

"You forget I can drive! I was taught in Austria by my family. They were all excellent drivers."

"Not in the BMW?" John was horrified at the prospect of Lutzi careering along the narrow, twisting roads around the lakes, and then speeding on the

Trans Canada Highway.

"Why not? I pay for it!" Lutzi asserted. "I shall certainly drive to this Antigonish in the BMW!"

Lutzi strutted around the room in triumph. John knew when he was beaten. There was nothing he could do except take cover, and count the hours until his departure.

~

When Rod got back from work that night, Roberta told him there was something she needed to discuss with him. But with the children needing help with their homework, and one thing and another, the opportunity was missed and Rod retired to bed early. So, she set her alarm for the crack of dawn in order to waylay him before he went to work.

She caught him in the bathroom, shaving. "Good morning, Roddie."

"You up already? What do you want?"

"Why should I want something?"

"You usually do, when you call me 'Roddie.'"

"I can't fool you, can I?"

Rod gave her a big grin surrounded by shaving cream. He reached out and hugged her tightly, wiping the cream off on her face.

"Uggh!" She recoiled. "You big brute!"

"Come on, what is it? Tell Roddie all about it."

"I want the day off tomorrow," Roberta answered quickly. "And the night."

"The plot thickens," said Rod portentously. "Would I be even remotely close if I guessed this had something to do with the dashing Sedgemoor?"

"You would." Roberta said with a smile. "He needs to go to England for a few weeks. I said I would drive him to Sydney to get a flight to Halifax."

"Ah. You could come straight back."

"I could."

"But you won't."

"No, I won't."

"So, Sydney, Nova Scotia is the designated place for the dirty deed to take place? Romantic downtown Sydney!"

"Don't you dare say it like that," she said, punching him in the arm. "There won't be anything dirty about it."

Deliberately keeping her waiting for an answer, Rod made a big show of washing his face, brushing his teeth, and putting on his plaid work shirt. Roberta waited, impatiently shifting her weight from foot to foot.

"Well?" she prompted.

"Okay," he said. "I'll make arrangements for Mrs. MacInnes from down the road to be here when the kids get home from school."

"Good. Thanks."

"But, you going to have get back here the next morning to give them breakfast."

"I can do that," she said grateful for what she could get. "If I left at five I could be here by seven easily."

"That's cutting it a bit fine," said Rod. "What if you ran into trouble on the road?"

"Damn!" She immediately saw how risky that scenario could be.

"Tell you what: I'll square it at work to go in late."

"God bless you, big brother!" Roberta gave him a big kiss on the cheek. "You're a marvel!"

"But you must be back here by ten at the latest. Promise?"

"I promise," she said.

21: To bed

The appointed day was as fine as any they had experienced this fall. The bright sun was already highlighting the orange and salmon-pink leaves, and splashes of blood red were now more frequent. Squadrons of small birds were gathering on telephone lines, while a pair of bald eagles per-formed a graceful aerobatic display high above. The smell of wood smoke was in the air. Everything pointed to this being a day like no other.

Full of trepidation, Roberta drove up to John's yard, parked, got out and tip-toed to the back door. This was insane, she thought. What if Lutzi caught them and started a frenetic rant? What if she threw plates and even knives at them? Why couldn't John have somehow lugged his suitcases to the road? Surely, they could not be that heavy.

Her heart pounding, she eased the door open and gingerly put her head round. Just inside the door, she could see that John's suitcases were all ready to go.

Softly she stepped inside and crept into the kitchen.

John was at the stove, stirring a pot.

"Hi" she whispered. "Is the coast clear?"

"Hi, sweetheart," said John giving her a quick kiss. "It's okay, she's upstairs, dead to the world. She took one of her Zopiclone last night. It knocks her out for hours."

"Let's get out of here. I feel like a criminal. Are you ready to roll?"

John turned off the stove and moved the pot to one side.

"I've made a stew for Lutzi's supper. She can't cook worth a damn. It's kind of a peace offering, not that it will do any good."

"Smells wonderful," said Roberta sniffing appreciatively. "What's in it?"

"Deer meat," said John. "Randy gave it to me. He just got a big buck up behind Dallas Brook."

"Any of those lovely mushrooms?"

"Yes, one or two. Grab that quiche." John pointed to one on the counter. "We can have it for lunch as a picnic."

"Let's go before she wakes," said Roberta putting the quiche in a bag.

"Right. Let's pretend we're eloping!"

Softly giggling, they picked up the cases and skulked out.

As they pulled out on to the road and headed east, Roberta felt the worry and tension fall away. They were free, she thought, they were together, and the day was theirs!

"I feel I've just escaped from Alcatraz," said John.

"I was wondering," said Roberta with a sly smile, "do you think we might just find time for something other than driving sometime today?"

"I think it's a distinct possibility," he replied, flashing her a huge grin. "We'll just have to see what opportunities present themselves."

She tipped her head back and sang:

> *I'll be loving you always,*
> *With a love that's true always.*
> *When the things you've planned*
> *Need a helping hand,*
> *I will understand always.*
>
> *Days may not be fair always,*
> *That's when I'll be there always.*
> *Not for just an hour,*
> *Not for just a day,*
> *Not for just a year, but always.*

John grinned and tried to join in, but had no great singing voice, so instead he beat time on the top of the dashboard. They dissolved into laughter.

They drove up through Big Harbour Centre, then Valley Mills, Orangedale and Iron Mines to the Trans Canada Highway, then off again at Aberdeen. Roberta had insisted on taking this roundabout route because it involved going on the Little Narrows ferry. She had always found the ferry to be romantic, and she especially liked the idyllic view of the little white church behind them as they crossed.

She remembered having come this way with her father when she was a little girl. She had told him she was going to be married in that church. He said that wasn't possible because she was Catholic and the church was Presbyterian. She asked him if they would allow it if she gave them money. Her father had laughed like water gurgling down a drain, telling her they would have to wait until the time came.

Now, she wondered if she would ever be married and, if so, would it ever be possible to fulfill that girlhood dream.

Although the crossing only took five minutes, she made John jump out and hang over the gunwale with her, watching the water bubbling around the sides of the boat. Then they climbed back into her car and were delighted to hear the clumpety-clump as they came off the ramp. In minutes they were on their way to Iona.

They spent a pleasant hour looking through the Highland Village in Iona, then poked about in the St. Columba cemetery, searching for the Gillis name on headstones because Roberta recalled being told some of her ancestors had settled thereabouts. The weather was unseasonably hot, and bees were buzzing about the flowers still blooming.

When they got back into the car, Roberta drove over the impressive Grand Narrows Bridge over the Barra Strait. The bridge had been built in 1993, but Roberta always thought of it as "new" because, when she had come this way with her father, it had not yet been constructed and this, too, required crossing by ferry boat.

Thoughts of her father came flooding back. Robert Gillis had been a bluff, jovial man who had seemed enormous to the young Roberta, whom he would swing in the air and balance on his shoulder. She had adored him, and suffered very keenly when he was taken from them in a forestry accident.

His hearing had been impaired for some years prior to his death, and he tried to hide it from his family and fellow workers. He had not heard the warning cry, and had been crushed by a twenty-meter pine tree.

What would he have thought of me today? she wondered. Would he disapprove?

Her father had been a strong Catholic and had lived strictly according to morality as defined by the Church, but she had a sneaking feeling that he might have turned a blind eye to her transgressions. At least, she hoped so.

After a while, they decided it was time for their picnic lunch, so, turning off on to a narrow, very rutted, dirt track they found a secluded glade, an opening in the woods where long grass, still lush and green, interspersed with ferns.

There in this earthly paradise they ate the quiche, drank some rather warm wine John had brought and, as the sun dappled through the trees, their relationship took the step for which they had so long waited.

Late in the afternoon they leisurely wound their way along the coast of St. Andrews Channel through Pipers Cove, the Mi'kmaq reserve at Eskasoni, Northside East Bay and eventually to Sydney, where they checked in to a curiously-named hotel, the Spanish Bay Inn, on the Esplanade.

Arm in arm they wandered along the waterfront, watching children rollerblading and seniors fishing in the harbour. Later, they went out for dinner and both had lobster.

John ordered Champagne, but the waiter said they didn't stock it, so he settled for a bottle of L'Acadie Blanc which had been made at the Eileanan Breagha winery near Marble Mountain, where they had come from that day. They agreed that they would pay a visit to the winery before the season was out and pick up more of their products.

Roberta was buoyant, happy, free and full of love. She had not had much experience of love in her forty years. Apart from fumbles after parties, she had enjoyed few relationships, and only two which could have been described as serious.

The first, Alistair MacMaster, was a local boy of nineteen when she herself was just seventeen. He went to Grande Cache, Alberta, to look for work and never came back.

The second, Ted, was a fellow police officer, tall, devastatingly handsome, with amazing technique. However, apart from police work, all he was interested in was sex, hockey and baseball. He had proudly declared to her that he had never read a book cover to cover, and never been to see a play. He thought poetry was "artsy fartsy" and that opera was complete madness. The only films he would watch were action or crime movies, and he thought that, unless it was about sports, conversation was a waste of time and energy.

Ted lasted a little under a year. She stuck it out with him for the sex, and because it fed her ego to be seen with a trophy boyfriend who turned other women's heads when they went out together.

This was certainly different from what it had been like with Ted. Of her relationship with Alistair, she could hardly remember many details, but she was sure it had not been anything like this, either. She was certain she had never felt this way before. This, she told herself, must be, was, the real thing.

Where it would lead, she didn't know and, at least for now, she did not care. She resolved to live for the moment and worry about the future when it happened.

In that glowing, contented frame of mind she went back to the hotel and to bed with John.

22: No secret

The harsh, unwelcome rasping of the alarm woke Roberta from a warm, sensual sybaritic haven. It was seven o'clock. She knew she didn't have to leave that early, but she was conscious of her promise to Rod, and wanted to take no chances in case there was trouble on the road.

She kissed John, reminded him to arrange for a taxi to take him to the airport, then gathered her few belongings and very reluctantly exited. She let herself out of the back door on to the hotel's strange, hidden parking lot and eased her car on to the Esplanade.

She cruised along Kings Road, on to the 125, then the 223. The road took her through Boisdale, Beaver Cove and Christmas Island, the legendary place from which thousands all over the world had tried to send Christmas cards stamped with the location. She was elated and sang like a linnet.

It had to be you
It had to be you
I wandered around, and I finally found
The somebody who
Could make me be true
And could make me be blue
And even be glad
Just to be sad—thinking of you
For nobody else gave me a thrill
With all your faults, I love you still
It had to be you
Wonderful you
It had to be you

Roberta did the 130 kilometres in just under two hours. She surprised Rod, who was sitting at the kitchen table, drinking coffee.

"The wanderer returns!" he cried. "You're early. Things must have not worked out."

"I didn't want to break my promise to you, big brother," she said, then pointedly added, "And no, things worked out just fine!"

"Ah," said Rod, "now I look at you, I see you are like new hen's egg."

"A new hen's egg?"

"Yeah. Just been laid!" Rod hooted.

She chased him around the kitchen as he warded off blows. They both laughed heartily.

"You can get off to work now," she said. "I'll see you tonight about five-thirty."

Rod grabbed his gear and headed for his truck.

There was very little housework to be done, so Roberta made herself a coffee and read the previous day's paper. When she had finished her coffee, she literally did not know what to do with herself.

She went up to see her mother several times, but there was nothing apparent that the old lady needed. The day ahead seemed empty without John, and the prospect of some thirteen or fourteen similar days was not an appealing one.

She went to the window and gazed out. On the other side of West Bay, she could just see some of the cottages at Lake Point, but could not tell if any of them were still occupied. She suspected they would have been closed and shuttered for the winter many weeks ago. Apart from the silver birches which retained their lemon colour, most hardwood trees were now either gold or orange, although increasingly, brilliant reds were more frequent.

Suddenly, out of nowhere, an American Kestrel landed on the deck rail and, holding its head on one side, appeared to be staring at her. What a magnificent creature, she thought, with its tawny chest, bluish head and rich brown back. Usually, they didn't see many kestrels in this area and she wondered where it had come from, where its mate was, and where it would go next.

She fancied that the two of them had established eye contact and that there was a battle of wills between them. So she kept staring, not daring to move a muscle. Then it was gone! Aha, she had won the contest!

She wondered what John was doing. He was likely on his way to Halifax by now, and then on to London on the overnight flight.

Roberta hated air travel. It made her tired and cranky. The seats were never comfortable and the air always seemed stale, and all the lining up was demoralizing. She thought of him dragging himself off the plane, lining up to get his car and driving to Bristol. Poor John, he'll be exhausted, she thought.

To fill the rest of the day, Roberta thought she would make the family a special supper. In the freezer she found a prime rib which she figured would have just enough time to thaw if she immersed it in cold water, so she decided they would have roast beef, mashed turnips and Yorkshire pudding, with a rich gravy.

She busied herself laying out pots and pans and arranging ingredients, all the while singing up a storm.

> *No one here can love or understand me*
> *Oh, what hard luck stories they all hand me*
> *Pack up all my cares and woe, here I go,*
> *winging low*
> *Bye, bye, blackbird.*
> *Where somebody waits for me*
> *Sugar's sweet, so is she*
> *Bye, bye, blackbird*

When the children tumbled into the house, they found her jolly and melodious. When they had shed their shoes, coats and school bags, and had changed, they trooped into the kitchen, enticed by the savoury odours. As they crowded around the table, Roberta enumerated the bill of fare.

"Yum!" said Bonnie, punching the air.

"Sounds okay," Brad said, sounding somewhat surprised that the menu met with his approval.

"I like that pudding stuff," said Angie, sweetly,

"But first," Roberta said, "you have to sing for your supper!"

"Yeah," said Bonnie, poking a groaning Brad.

"Oh yes please," Angie bounced up and down on her chair. "Can we do *The Wheels on the Bus*? Please."

"That is exactly what I had in mind," said Roberta.

"With spoons!"

They cheered again and rattled their spoons on the table.

"Angie, you go first."

> *The wipers on the bus go swish, swish, swish;*
> *Swish, swish, swish;*
> *Swish, swish, swish.*
> *The wipers on the bus go swish, swish, swish,*
> *all through the town.*

"Now you, Bonnie."

> *The horn on the bus goes beep, beep, beep;*
> *Beep, beep, beep;*
> *Beep, beep, beep.*
> *The horn on the bus goes beep, beep, beep,*
> *all through the town.*

"Come on, Brad. It's your turn."

> *The money on the bus goes, clink, clink, clink;*
> *Clink, clink, clink;*
> *Clink, clink, clink.*
> *The money on the bus goes, clink, clink, clink,*
> *all through the town.*

"And all together now! With spoons!"

> *The baby on the bus says "Wah, wah, wah;*
> *Wah, wah, wah;*
> *Wah, wah, wah."*
> *The baby on the bus says "Wah, wah, wah,"*
> *all through the town.*

"What the hell is going on here?" Rod demanded, bursting into the room. "What's all this about?"

"Wah! Wah! Wah!" they all shouted at him pounding the table with their utensils.

"We're having roast beef with the pudding stuff," Angie cheerfully informed her father.

"Sounds wonderful," said Rod. "What's the occasion, and why is everyone so chipper?"

"She's been with her luvveur," drawled Bonnie theatrically.

"Shush now," Rod directed. "That's a secret."

"It's no secret," Brad asserted. "Everyone knows she's been with her boyfriend."

Roberta quickly turned away, blushing to the roots of her hair. She frantically stirred the gravy.

Rod promptly rushed to the rescue. "Stop all this nonsense immediately! I'm starving. For the love of Pete, let's eat."

23: Thinking of him

The days dragged on. The weather stayed magnificent, although colder. Roberta felt it was being wasted without John.

Her longing for his return was in no way assuaged when an old problem came back with a vengeance. Ever since she was a teenager, Roberta had suffered from excruciating leg cramps, not only in her gastrocnemius like most other people, but also in all the other muscles of the legs; the soleus, biceps, tibialis and extensors. Some nights the cramps would keep her awake for hours, and often she found even standing in very hot water brought no relief.

Medical research had not advanced at all in this area, the doctors offering no suggestions as to either cause or cure. She had tried all the so-called home cures and had found them all to be old wives' tales.

She had even Googled the most recent medical study of the problem, and discovered, after ploughing through the mountains of medical jargon, that they had reached no firm conclusions as to the reasons for cramps, and none on treatment. They said cramps were most likely caused by "an underlying condition", but did not specify what that condition could be.

She determined that the problem was related to the changing of the seasons, the worst attacks coming in late October and early November and again in April/May.

Curiously, she had heard that in the vineyards of Bordeaux when, in spring, the sap started to rise in the vines, so simultaneously the wine in the barrels in the cellar began its secondary fermentation. She couldn't draw a direct connection between the two situations, but it did raise the question in her mind as to how the wine and her legs knew when it was time to react! With such speculations she whiled away the time.

One morning she decided to go down to see Dan. The air was chilly, and the road was littered with brown and yellow leaves. Here and there branches were naked, yet in other places they bore masses of impenetrable scarlet, so bright it was almost as if someone had used DayGlo paint.

About halfway down the hill, Roberta thought she saw someone moving behind the trunk of an old oak. She stopped and stared into the foliage. "You sick bastard!" she shouted, "you don't scare me! Come on out. Show yourself!"

She waited for another minute, then decided that in the riotous confusion of the fall colours she could easily have been mistaken. She bent down to pick up a branch which the wind had blown across the road, and hurled it in the direction of the oak, then she carried on down the hill.

When she got to Dan's place, she found him getting ready to go out in his truck. He wound the window down.

"Hey, Sergeant," she called. "Heading for town?"

"Hello, Sergeant," said Dan, "No, I'm heading up to the old quarry workings. Want to come?"

"Sure." Roberta climbed into the passenger seat.

"I want to get a chunk of marble," Dan explained. "I thought it might be nice as a door stop after I've trimmed and polished it."

They parked off the road and ambled into the old quarry, shuffling through the fallen leaves, Roberta kicking them high into the air just as she had as a little girl.

"How about that one?" She pointed to a white surface showing through the leaf cover.

"I suspect that will be too big," said Dan, probing it with his boot. "It's not bad, but it's too heavy. We could never carry it to the truck."

They sat down on a huge rock outcrop. Dan took out his cigarettes and offered her one, but she refused. She knew from bitter experience that, no matter how tempting it might be, no matter how much she might say it was just this once, she could so easily get hooked again.

Squinting, Roberta looked up through the overhead canopy, a kaleidoscope of many shades with a multitude of flashes of light from the sun.

"I can tell you're thinking of Sedgemoor, aren't you?"

"Yes."

"You miss him, don't you?"

"Yes."

"He's only been gone five minutes and already you miss him."

She nodded.

"I wish to God you felt the same way about me!" Dan sounded as if he were in pain.

"Let's go and find your rock," said Roberta firmly, knowing nothing she could say or do could offer him any consolation.

24: Moving Mrs. Gillis

To her inexpressible joy, the next day Roberta received a phone call from John. Her heart was pounding when she heard his rich baritone over the line, a voice which had become so special to her.

"My darling. Are you alright?"

"Yes, I'm fine. Missing you terribly."

"Me, too. You have no idea how much. Are you at your brother's place?"

"Yes. My aunt's estate is in an awful mess. It's taking forever to sort out. Every time we think we've got it settled, the lawyers come up with another legal step which has to be completed."

"It sounds tedious."

"Very tedious. It's all about waiting," John complained.

"But you'll be back home on schedule?"

"Oh yes, I'm sure of that."

"I'll be counting the days," said Roberta with great feeling.

"And I'll be counting the hours. Have to go now, sweetheart. Another meeting with the lawyers."

"Okay. Love you."

"Love you too," said John solemnly.

The day after John's call, Roberta received another. This time it was from Agnes Matheson, the Care Coordinator from Social Services. "Ms. Gillis. Everything is ready for your mother, if you want to bring her in."

"Oh, thank you. That's marvellous. When can she come?"

"Tomorrow. In the morning would be best," said Mrs. Matheson, business-like as usual.

"We'll be there."

"Good. And, Ms. Gillis, once you hand her over, so to speak, we prefer if you don't hang around fussing. We find it better that way, both for the staff and the patient."

"All right." Roberta was rather miffed at the suggestion that she might 'hang around fussing', but thought it better to let it slide. "I'll see you tomorrow."

"Goodbye, Ms. Gillis," said Mrs. Matheson, hanging up without further ado.

Roberta thought she should go up and inform her mother of what had been decided. She knew it would not register with the old lady, but she felt it was the proper thing to do.

When she crept into the room, Mrs. Gillis was in her usual place, rocking away.

"Hello Ma. I've come to tell you that you'll be going to a new home tomorrow."

There was not, could not be, any response.

"I'll think you'll like it there. I hope you will."

Nothing, but rock-rock-rock was her answer.

"I love you, Ma."

Roberta threw her arms around her mother, kissed her, then sank to her knees. It almost seemed as if they were one, rocking with the motion of the chair.

Roberta sang softly:

When your hair is silver white
And your cheeks no longer bright,
With the roses of the May,
I will kiss your cheek and say:
Oh! my dearest, mine alone, alone,
You have never older grown.
Dearest, you are growing old,
Silver threads among the gold,
Shine upon your brow today,
Life is fading fast away.

When she tiptoed out of the room, the tears were

streaming down her cheeks.

Rod and Roberta had decided that it would be best if the moving of the old lady was not carried out while the children were around, so the next day she waited until they had gone to school before she started to organize the task.

Mrs. Matheson had told her that the number of personal items Mrs. Gillis could take with her was limited, and she had great difficulty in deciding what to select. Finally, when she had determined upon a few essentials, she took them down and stowed them in the car, then with considerable trepidation went up to get her mother.

Roberta did not know exactly why, but she expected resistance from her mother, that it would be a struggle to get her downstairs and out into the car. Nothing could have been further from the truth as the old lady meekly took her daughter's hand and docilely descended the stairs.

At the bottom, it was almost as if the old lady had remembered where the car was kept because, without assistance, she turned and headed for the yard. She was easily nestled into the passenger seat, allowing the seat belt to be buckled around her without question. Then they were away.

The installation of her mother in the nursing home was a lot quicker and less trouble than she had anticipated. After signing a form (which she later described to Rod as 'the receipt'), the staff seemed anxious to hustle her out of the building.

She said a quick 'goodbye' to her mother, kissed her on the forehead, then was gone, experiencing a mixture of relief and guilt. She made her way back, rejoined the TransCanada Highway, crossed the Canso Causeway, and headed for the town of Antigonish.

25: A death on Main Street

A small university town in the northeast of mainland Nova Scotia, Antigonish was quaint but busy. Today the streets were filled with residents and students.

It was not exactly a modern metropolis, so Roberta did not expect to find high fashion in the stores. But she discovered more than a few items which she liked in some shops, and enjoyed looking in the windows of others.

Arms full of bags, she was making her way back to the car when her gaze was arrested by a vehicle which looked exactly like John's BMW. She crossed the street and peered in through the windows and, seeing his fire-fighting gear in the back, knew it was the same vehicle.

So, she thought, apparently Lutzi carried out her promise, or threat, to seize the car and go on the town.

Roberta shrugged and moved on, resolved that if she should see the other woman in the distance she would cross the street or hide in a doorway. The last thing she needed today was another loud, accusatory confrontation in a public place.

As Roberta continued to saunter along Main Street glancing in store windows, she noticed a commotion on the other side. A circle of people were standing on the sidewalk, talking excitedly and staring at the ground. An RCMP police constable rushed across in front of her and pushed his way through the bystanders.

Instantly, Roberta was in her police mode and, curious as to what had occurred, walked over. As she approached, she could see that what the people were gaping at was a body. When she got closer, she poked her head over the shoulder of the woman in front of her and looked down at the body.

It was Lutzi Sedgemoor.

Roberta was frozen to the spot, her mind reeling. Lutzi looked as if she were dead and, when an ambulance arrived and the paramedics handled the body, she heard them say that the woman had expired.

When the ambulance had pulled away, she walked up to the RCMP officer and asked him where they were taking Lutzi's corpse. On hearing that it would be taken to Saint Martha's Hospital, Roberta identified herself as a fellow officer and asked if she could accompany him.

At first he seemed reluctant, and frowned as he examined her warrant card as if searching for a reason not to grant her request. "Toronto," he said slowly, as if he had not met the word before. "You're way out of your jurisdiction."

"I know," Roberta said, smiling sweetly, "but, you see, I knew the deceased. She was my neighbour in Lime Hill."

"Lime Hill? You from Nova Scotia?"

"Born and bred. Moved to Toronto about ten years ago."

"Why didn't you say? That's different. I'm Ralston McVicar. I grew up just up the road in Scottsville."

"Small world," Roberta said. "I'm Bobby."

"You'd better jump in, Bobby," Ralston said, holding open the front passenger-side door of the RCMP cruiser. "We'll see what they have to say. My guess is a heart attack. Those people said she just collapsed. Don't know what else would do that to a person."

"Me neither," Roberta said thoughtfully. "I know she complained a lot about her health, but I never heard that she had any kind of heart condition."

"We'll soon find out."

By the time they got to the hospital they were like old pals. She followed Ralston into a holding area and they waited, chatting, for a report on Lutzi.

Shortly, a gray-haired, middle-aged physician entered. "Hello, I'm Dr. Carl Francis," he said. "And you are…?"

"This is Constable MacVicar and I'm Roberta Gillis."

"Are you related to the deceased?"

"No I'm not. As I explained to the constable, I'm a neighbour. Her husband is in England and, as far as I know, the only other relatives are nieces somewhere in Austria."

"Do you know how Mr. Sedgemoor can be reached?"

"Yes, I have a telephone number for his brother in Bristol."

"I think that, under the circumstances," Dr. Francis said, "you should call him and let him know his wife is dead. It might be better than the hospital calling. Or the police."

Constable MacVicar nodded his assent. "Do you mind doing that, Ms. Gillis?"

"No, I'll do it," Roberta replied. "What should I tell him? I mean, how did she die?"

"Ah, well, there you have me," the doctor said. "At the moment, we have no idea."

"No idea at all?"

"Unfortunately not. I say 'unfortunately' because, where the cause of death is not apparent, we're required…"

"To conduct a post mortem," interrupted Roberta, "I know."

When the doctor showed surprise, Roberta produced her warrant card again. "I'm a detective sergeant with the Toronto Police."

Ralston MacVicar nodded solemnly, as if to suggest to the doctor that Roberta was not anybody to be treated lightly.

"Good God," exclaimed Dr. Francis. "Well, you'll know the drill, then, won't you?"

"When will you be able to conduct the autopsy?"

"Well, I won't be doing it, of course, but I had a word with the pathologist on my way down here. She says that once she gets the official request, she can do it any time."

"I'll attend to the paper work," said Ralston.

"Thank you. Considering all the circumstances I think we might allow you to observe, if you would like to." Roberta nodded vigorously. "If that is all right with the RCMP."

"I'll check it out with my Staff Sergeant," said Ralston, "but I can't see it will be a problem if it's all right with the medical people."

~

Roberta made a quick call to Rod to explain the

situation and to ask if he could leave work early so as to look after the children when they got home from school. Stunned by the news, he agreed at once. "Jesus! Who'd have thought it? She just dropped dead just like that! In the street?"

"It would seem so. I didn't see it happen. I came on the scene later."

"Well, I guess you'd better stay and find out what did her in. I'll make sure I'm back in time for the kids."

"Thanks, Roddie. See you later tonight. I can't say when."

"OK. See you, sis."

~

Some hours later the pathologist was ready to commence.

Suitably gowned, Roberta, Ralston, the pathologist, Dr. MacKenna, and her assistant, Nurse Candow, assembled around the slab on which Lutzi's naked body was lying. Scattered around were stainless steel containers to hold various organs and bloodied instruments.

Every step she took, and every discovery she made, the pathologist announced into a microphone. Finally, she ripped off her gloves, threw them in the trash and washed her hands at the sink.

"Sorry to bore you with the running commentary," said Dr. MacKenna. "It's to provide an instantaneous record of the procedure and its findings. How much of it were you able to follow?"

"I got the general drift. In good general health—"

"Except for total renal failure and some lesser damage to the liver. The cortex of the kidneys is extremely swollen, which would indicate acute tubular necrosis."

She picked up the container and showed the kidneys to Roberta.

"Uggh! What could have caused that?"

"The most likely cause of this tissue picture would be toxicity, "said Dr. MacKenna. "She may have drunk something particularly potent and nasty. A tox screen should tell us what, if anything, we're dealing with."

"Will you have a screen done?" asked Roberta.

"Oh yes, it's definitely indicated."

"Will you let me know the results?"

"Sure, I'll call both you and Constable MacVicar if you leave your phone numbers."

"Thank you, doctor. At least now I will have something to tell Mr. Sedgemoor when I call him."

"There is one other puzzling aspect to this case."

"Oh? What is that?"

"If she received attention earlier, I imagine there would have been a chance of saving her. You see, it's highly likely that this woman would have suffered for some time. A few days anyway, I would have thought. She probably would have experienced a loss of appetite, fatigue, dizziness and extreme discomfort. What I don't understand is why didn't she go to a physician."

"I think I know the answer to that," Roberta offered. "She was a foreigner and thought all the doctors in this country are fools. I heard her say as much on one occasion."

"Well we're not fools," said Dr. MacKenna. "It just feels like that sometimes."

As she drove back from Antigonish late that night, Roberta was both shaken and thoughtful. She was so conflicted she didn't know how to react. On the one hand, it seemed a veritable Godsend that John would now be free, but even thinking that way made her feel horribly guilty.

In this confused state of mind she pulled into the yard to find the house in darkness, all but the porch light. Rod had gone to bed leaving a scrawled note on the kitchen table, telling her he had to leave very early the next morning.

Her mind still racing with images of bodies on sidewalks, swollen, bloody kidneys, and Lutzi's belly

and breasts bisected by an enormous incision, Roberta went straight to bed.

26: From stem to stern

The next morning, when Roberta got the children's breakfast she was still in something of a daze. Naturally, they were full of questions about what they saw as a great adventure.

Rod had filled them in to some extent, but Bonnie and Brad indulged a macabre curiosity for more details. Only Angie showed no interest in the neighbourhood's latest sensation, and played quietly with her colouring book.

"Did she just drop dead on the sidewalk?" Bonnie asked.

"Yes."

"Did you find her?"

"No."

"Dad says you went back to the hospital where they cut her open. Is that right?"

"Yes." Roberta was tired and had no wish to relive it, but the children were relentless.

"Was she naked like on *Silent Witness*?" Bonnie

asked.

"Yes."

"Yeah, but you could see *everything*, right?" Brad added.

"Yes, you little pervert," said Roberta taking a swipe at him.

"Did you see the doctor cut her open," Bonnie paused for theatrical effect, "from *stem to stern*?"

"Yes."

"Was there blood *everywhere*?" asked Brad with relish.

"Enough, you little ghouls! Go to school before I cut *you* open from stem to stern!"

She chased them out and watched them climb on to the bus.

A little later, after Mrs. MacLeod had collected Angie, Roberta went upstairs and was almost to the top step when it struck her that her mother was no longer there. She felt very sad and, strangely, very lonely.

Despite the fact that the old lady had not communicated with any of them in several years, made no sounds, and never left her room, her presence was always felt in the house. Now there was something of a vacuum; something quite central was missing.

The telephone ringing shook her out of her reverie, and she ran down to answer it in the kitchen.

"Hello, Sergeant Gillis? It's Dr. MacKenna calling."

"Oh, hi, Doctor. Thanks for calling. Do you have any news?"

"I have the report back on the tox screen, but I'm afraid we're none the wiser. High potassium levels and acidosis would lend support to my original guess, but the screen hasn't identified anything. They checked for all the usual suspects—alcohols, opiates and so on—and even plugged in a special screen for heavy metals, but nothing showed up. I guess it's one of those mysteries we sometimes encounter. I sorry we couldn't be more helpful. You'll just have to tell Mr. Sedgemoor that we just don't know why his poor wife died."

"That is so weird," Roberta said, "but thank you anyway for all your help. I am very grateful to you, and I am sure Mr. Sedgemoor will be, too."

Now came the difficult task of telling John about Lutzi's demise. She had no idea how he would take the news. Would he be calm or devastated?

She had delayed calling him because it would have been the middle of the night in Bristol, but also because she wanted something concrete to tell him. Dr. MacKenna had confirmed that there was nothing specific to tell about the cause of death, so she could put it off no longer.

After exchanging the usual fond pleasantries, she jumped right in. "John, prepare yourself for a shock. Lutzi's dead."

"What? For a minute, there, I thought you said she was dead."

"Yes, she is dead. She dropped dead in the street yesterday in Antigonish."

There was a very long silence.

"What happened, Bobby?"

"They don't know."

"What do you mean, they don't know?" John sounded incredulous.

"They did a post-mortem and ran a tox screen, but they couldn't find anything."

"This is like something out of a nightmare," said John. "There has to be a reason why somebody drops dead. Did they find nothing wrong with her heart?"

"Nothing," she said.

"I just can't get my head around this, Bobby." John sounded dazed. "It's all so unbelievable."

"I know. I don't know what to say. I can't honestly say I'm sorry she's....out of the way...but not like this."

"It's is hard not to be in two minds about it, I admit. Look, I'll come home as soon as I can."

"Of course," said Roberta. "You'll let me know when you have the details of the flights?"

"Sure."

"Okay, sweetheart. I look forward to seeing you soon."

"Me, too. Love you."

"Love you, too."

And he was gone. She had never been to Bristol and had no idea what kind of a place it was. She wondered what kind of house his brother had, and whether John would have taken the call in front of them or sitting on the stairs outside the room. She pictured John's brother and sister-in-law hovering around him wondering what on earth had happened.

When she thought more about it, she realized that she knew very little about John's brother, not what he was like nor what he did for a living. She imagined he was a professional man of some kind, living on a road in a black and white mock Tudor house in a leafy suburb, and that his wife was a smartly dressed woman in her forties who was in business of some sort, possibly banking or the stock market. Do they have children, she wondered, and, if so, how old would they be?

27: Accusation

The news of Lutzi's sudden death had gone around the neighbourhood like wildfire. There was scarcely a person in Lime Hill, Marble Mountain and even West Bay who did not already have some version of how the crazy woman who had broken up the Mac-Donalds' benefit dinner had met her untimely end. So, naturally when Roberta visited Dan that day, the subject of their conversation was a foregone conclusion.

He was wandering around the edges of his lawn, dead-heading the remaining flowers and tossing them into an old wheelbarrow. Hands in pockets, Roberta followed him around.

"You say the tox screen was completely clear?"

"Well, they couldn't find anything. So it couldn't have been anything common, you know, like disinfectant or anti-freeze, or anything like that."

"Medical science baffled," pronounced Dan as if he were reading a newspaper headline.

"I don't know but there is the possibility she had some insidious disease which lingered for years undetected. Then it finally caught up with her."

Dan put his secateurs in his back pocket, wiped the back of his neck with a handkerchief, stretched, and then lit up a cigarette. "How did lover boy take it when you told him?"

"You'd better drop the sarcasm or I'm out of here!" said Roberta, "He was very rattled, naturally. What do you expect? His wife has just died."

"When's he coming back?" Dan asked, ignoring Roberta's admonition.

"Tomorrow. I'm going to pick him up."

Dan put his foot up on the wheelbarrow to tie a shoelace which had come undone. He paused for a few seconds, then sniffed. "Kind of convenient, wasn't it?

"What was?" demanded Roberta, "What the hell do you mean?"

"Well, look at it objectively, as if you were investigating a case. He falls in love with you and you fall in love with him. Then his wife dies under mysterious circumstances."

"You prick!" Roberta turned on him. "What are you implying? Are you saying what I think you're saying?"

Dan slowly took a drag on his cigarette, dropped

the butt, then purposefully ground it into the dirt. "I don't know what I'm saying, Bobby."

"Jesus, Danny, that's sick! I've heard of jealousy but this is beyond the pale! Besides, John was forty-eight hundred kilometres away when it happened."

"Yeah, he's in the clear, I guess," said Dan with a sly smile. "But what if he had an accomplice here?"

"What?!"

"What *were* you doing in Antigonish that day, any-way?"

Roberta's brain nearly popped out of her head and she fell upon Dan, flailing and punching him furiously. "You bastard!" she shouted. "You son of a bitch!"

Half hurting, half laughing, Dan fell to the ground and rolled away from her. Angrily, Roberta stalked away, out of the driveway and up the hill.

"It's okay, Bobby," he called after her. "I won't arrest you. I'm retired, remember?"

Roberta stopped and turned back to him, snarling with rage. "Piss off, you swine!" she screamed at him. "You rotten bastard!"

28: Separate rooms

John's flight was due to land at Halifax's Stanfield airport just before one o'clock, so the next morning, not long after she had seen the children off to school, Roberta got into her car and headed south. Again, she had to prevail upon Rod to change his work arrangements, but he was as amenable as ever.

She reflected on what a wonderful brother she had, invariably supportive and understanding, but she could not avoid wondering if that was because they had seen each other so seldom over the years.

She made it to the airport in two hours and forty-five minutes, which meant that she had almost three quarters of an hour to wait before landing time. To kill the time, she made at least ten tours around the terminal, examining every mundane feature in great detail.

Airports are, she thought, among the most soul-destroying places on earth. Ordinary people, who would seem fine anywhere else, here took on the appearance of selfish, demanding monsters and degenerates, sweating, coughing, wheezing, and waddling along as if they could barely walk.

Finally, John's plane landed and she rushed to the exit from Customs and Immigration. Due to an elaborate computer procedure designed to improve security and passenger service, it now took twice as long for travellers to run the gauntlet and emerge to freedom as it had before the 'improvements' were made. This meant another wait of twenty minutes for Roberta before she saw an obviously exhausted John come through the door.

She threw herself at him, almost knocking him over. "God, I missed you," she said. "I missed you so much."

"Not half as much as I missed you," John replied, seizing her and kissing her over and over.

Having made something of an exhibition of themselves, they hastily moved out of the way of other passengers and went out to Roberta's car.

"Did you get your aunt's will straightened out?" she asked when they were on the highway.

"At long last. What a frigged-up situation. After all that rigmarole, we found that almost as much tax was owed as was in the residue of the estate, and then we had to pay legal fees. So I'm sorry, darling, if you thought I'd be coming home a rich man."

"That's okay, sweetheart. I never could handle luxury," said Roberta. "Oh, before I forget. You can pick up your car from the RCMP in Antigonish any time in the next few days."

"Good. I did wonder about that. Is it still in one piece?"

"It looked alright the last time I saw it. No scratches or dents."

"That's a miracle. Lutzi hadn't driven in years. I had visions of her smashing it up."

"We could make a detour to pick it up today, if you want." Roberta volunteered.

"No, let's get home," said John wearily, "I'm too tired to drive now. And I need your company."

Within a few minutes John fell asleep, so the rest of the journey Roberta had to endure in silence. He did not wake until she pulled the car into the Sedgemoors' yard.

Each carrying a suitcase, they struggled into the house. John dropped his case on the floor, switched on the lights and turned up the heating. He walked over to the drinks cabinet and poured them each a Scotch. They embraced again, sharing more kisses.

"You'll stay tonight, of course," John said tenderly.

"John, I don't feel right about it. I mean, not like this, so soon after....It seems kind of indecent."

"She's gone, Bobby, and nothing we do or say can

bring her back. She'll be just as dead next week, or next month, as she is now. We love each other, don't we? Let's not be hypocrites about it."

"I'm sorry, sweetheart, I couldn't, and not in the bed that you and she—"

"We had separate rooms, Bobby." John tried to be reassuring. "We hadn't...you know...done anything like that for years."

Bobby was wracked by highly-conflicting emotions. She desperately wanted to stay, but knew it was an affront to what she thought was right.

She hesitated for a minute before speaking again. "No, it's no use. I'm not comfortable with it now. Let's wait at least until the memorial service is over. That won't be too long to wait. Is that alright with you?"

"Of course it is," said John. "I understand. I've arranged the cremation for the day after tomorrow."

"She's being cremated?"

"Yes, I'll send the ashes to her nieces in Zisterdorf. Then she'll be back in the only place where she was ever happy."

"That's nice. I'm sure they'll appreciate that."

"I hope so," said John.

"I'm going to duck home now. I've been kind of neglecting the family of late. I'll see you at the service."

"Okay."

They hugged and kissed again several times before she tore herself away from him and headed on down the hill to the Gillis place.

She had gone only a few metres when there was a rustling in the bushes at the side of the road. She could not see anything, but she felt sure she had company again.

Who is this person and why is he or she—yes, she thought, it could be a she—persecuting me like this? What have I done to deserve this kind of treatment?

There was one consolation, she thought, and that was if the person intended anything violent, it was likely he—or she—would have done it by now.

"One of these days," she shouted, "I'm going to find out who you are and give you a damn good kicking!"

Silence and stillness were the only answer, which came on the gentle breeze which caressed the turning leaves of the trees.

29: Gossip

Up at the general store, Norman MacKenzie and Violet McIntosh were in the middle of a serious discussion. The mood was edgy and febrile.

"I think you're being too hard on the woman, Violet," Norman said. "I find her a very pleasant person to get along with."

"That's because you're an old fool where the young ones are concerned," shouted Gertie from the back of the store. "Spend all your time looking at their legs!"

"Huh, young ones!" Snorted Violet. "She's no spring chicken. Forty if she's a day. And her spreading stories about being spied on and followed! Who on earth would want to follow her, that's what I'd like to know."

"Ha!" yelled Gertie. "It's probably Norm who's spying on her. I sometimes wonders where he gets to of a night!"

"Take no notice, Violet," Norman said. "She's having the hot flushes again."

Just then, the bell over the front door rang loudly and Ida Ferguson entered. "Good day Norman. Good morning Vi," said Mrs. Ferguson and, calling to the back of the store, "Hello Gertie!"

"Hello Ida!"

"What's all the news?"

"Well, these two have been giving a good going-over to poor Roberta," replied Norman, "You know, Rod Gillis' sister."

"Poor Roberta indeed!" snorted Ida. "There's been nothing but trouble around here ever since she came back. Fires breaking out all over the place, she-nanigans with married men, staying late at men's trailers. Oh, I knows all about it!"

"Ida, my dear, surely you're not saying that she set those fires."

"I'm saying nothing about nobody, Norman, but just answer me this: when did them fires first break out? I'll tell you. 'Twas the day after she got here!"

"What's all this about married men?" inquired Vi-olet McIntosh.

"Where you been living, Violet?" Gertie chimed in from the store window, where she was balancing a stack of cans of beans. "You been living on Mars or something? She's been carrying on with that Sedge-moor fellow. Everybody knows that, girl."

"And Sedgemoor's dear wife not yet cold in the ground. Disgraceful, I call it," said Ida.

"No, you don't say! Indeed, not at all the proper way to behave," intoned Violet piously. "Even when she was a child I had my doubts about Roberta Gillis."

"I heard tell she was a lesbian," said Violet.

"That wouldn't surprise me either," said Norman, "after being in Toronto all these years."

"Norman MacKenzie," called out Gertie, "you wouldn't know whether your arse was punched or bored!"

30: Brown leaves underfoot

The day of Lutzi's memorial service was grey, cloudy and quite cold. Dark, ominous clouds brooded overhead. There were more brown leaves on the branches and a great many more underfoot and blowing about.

It was a very small group which gathered at the chapel. In fact only John, Roberta, Rod, Lolly, Lavender, Norman MacKenzie, The Fire Chief, and a Presbyterian minister were present. John had tried to get clergy who was Lutheran, the denomination in which Lutzi had grown up, but was unsuccessful, so a Reverend MacLean had kindly consented to fill in. Roberta felt embarrassed and deeply hypocritical for being there. As for others, they had neither known nor liked the deceased woman. The only person present who seemed to be genuinely grieving was John, whose mournful appearance cast despondency over the entire group.

Rev. MacLean said a few words of a very general

nature. He had never even met Lutzi, so could say nothing about her beyond platitudes. He had heard something of her nature, so did not even attempt to portray her as a loving wife and good neighbour. Instead, he devoted his few words to forgiveness, and how the Lord would welcome all manner of people into heaven.

After he had intoned the usual "ashes to ashes, dust to dust" invocation, the sound of piped organ music flooded the chapel, to be quickly followed by the roar of the retort as the coffin slowly disappeared through the asbestos drapes.

John shook hands with everyone, including Roberta, and thanked them all for coming. He stopped to give Rev. MacLean his fee, then joined Rod and Roberta in the parking lot.

"Thanks for everything," he said.

Rod looked extremely uncomfortable, jingling his keys in his pocket and shifting his weight from one foot to another. "I'll go and get the Cherokee," he said. "I'll bring her round and pick you up here. Do you need a drive, Mr. Sedgemoor?"

"Please, Rod, call me John. And thanks for the offer, but I have my own car. I picked it up in Antigonish yesterday."

"Oh, okay." Rod shambled away, kicking leaves as he went.

"Why didn't you say? I would have driven you." Roberta was put out.

"You've done enough. I got a ride with Norman. He had to go in to pick up some supplies."

"Oh."

"Will you come up tonight? About nine?"

"Try to stop me," she whispered.

31: Suspicion

Despite its large size, by the glow of the single lamp, John's bedroom seemed warm, safe and cozy. There was a rich Indian carpet on the floor and quality reproductions of Impressionist paintings on the walls. The large bed had bright blue silk sheets and large soft pillows. Roberta lay on her back with her eyes closed and a smile on her face. John lay on his side, propped up on one elbow, affectionately, protectively watching her. "So, how are you doing, Ms. Gillis?"

"Mmmm. Wonderful!" said Roberta, rolling over and kissing him. "I do love you so."

"I'm very glad to hear it. I love you, too. More than all the stars in the sky."

~

Thus it was that, every night from then on, Roberta

slipped away from the Gillis place after Rod had gone to bed, and every morning snuck back in before the children were up and about. She and John behaved as discreetly as they could under the circumstances, but everybody knew what was going on.

The MacDonalds encouraged her in their affair with jokes, grins and nudges. However, she got some strange, disapproving looks from others as she moved about the community. But she didn't care. Let them disparage her all they want. Some of their pejorative comments might smart, but she could endure them. She was in love.

There were no further fires in the community, which was a relief to everyone, and it seemed that the mysterious watcher had given up harassing her. The days became sharper, the nights colder. The yellows, oranges, pinks, salmons and reds which had covered the landscape with a blaze of colour had now disappeared. The whole of the land around the lakes which was not occupied by conifers now wore a mantle of portentous brown. Winter was on the way.

~

One night quite late, Roberta said she was thirsty and wanted a beer.

"There's some in the fridge," said John. "I'll go down and get you one."

"No, I'll go," Roberta said. She jumped out of bed and grabbed the quilt, wrapping it around herself. "I've got a cramp in my leg, so I need to walk about for at least fifteen minutes. Is there anything I can get for you while I'm down there?"

"Yes please, sweetheart. Would you get my reading glasses from the study?" John reached over to the side of the bed and picked up a slim volume. "I bought this book of romantic poems when I was in England. I want to read some of them to you."

"You are so sweet, I'd love to hear them when I get back."

She blew him a kiss as she left the bedroom and, clutching the quilt with one hand, descended the stairs to the kitchen. The house was in darkness, but a strong moon shone through the picture windows, making long, weird shadows where its light fell on various pieces of furniture.

She opened the fridge door, took out and un-capped a beer, and took a big gulp. She kicked the door shut, then wandered around the house trying to work out her cramp.

The house was tastefully and expensively furnished, but no room more so than John's study. There was a beautiful, polished rosewood desk, a big, soft, black leather swivel chair, gleaming brass lamps, and shelves filled to capacity with books of all descriptions. By the moonlight she could see that biography, politics, fictions and travel were all well represented. On the walls were photographs of a much younger John on the set of *Hampton Nights*, and one of him with an older man who she thought could have been his brother.

Roberta switched on the desk lamp, which cast a greenish glow over the surface. John's reading glasses, in their leather case, sat neatly beside a calendar and a notepad.

When Roberta reached for the glasses, the quilt started to slip, so, giggling, she grabbed it and pulled it back into position. Putting the beer bottle down, she picked up the glasses, and was about to turn away when her eye caught a book sticking out of one of the pigeon holes which held stationery. Idly, she picked it up and looked at the cover.

It was *The Audubon Society Field Guide to American Mushrooms*.

Noticing a piece of paper protruding from one of the pages, she removed it, and saw that it was covered with handwritten notes, entries like: "*Orellanine: gentilis? Speciosissimus*?"

Now looking at the page in the book which the slip was marking, she read the entry: *Cortinarius gentilis*. Deadly Cort.

When John shouted from upstairs, she almost jumped out of her skin.

"You alright, sweetheart? Can you find the glasses?"

"Yes," called back Roberta, flustered and shaky, "I've found them. I'm just walking off my cramp. Be there soon."

"Okay. Take your time."

Hastily turning back to the book, she flipped the page. Her heart almost stopped beating when she saw the entry.

> *Eating this mushroom and closely related species typically involves life-threatening kidney failure; symptoms usually do not appear until from three days to two weeks after ingestion.*

Her heart pounding, Roberta hurriedly replaced the book, grabbed her beer, switched off the lamp and went back upstairs.

Sitting in bed with her arms folded across her chest, Roberta stared blankly ahead while John read poem after poem, beautifully delivered in a lilting baritone, but none of a word of which did she hear or could have remembered. Instead her mind was racing. Snippets of past conversations and events came back to her like bolts from the blue.

> *"It's insidious and there's no antidote and no medical treatment."*
> *"John, what are we going to do?"*
> *"I don't know, Bobby. I'll think of something"*
> *"I've made a stew for Lutzi's dinner. She can't cook worth a damn."*
> *"Any mushrooms in here?"*
> *"One or two."*
> *"Kind of convenient isn't it. You fall in love with him and he falls in love with you. Then his wife dies under mysterious circumstances."*
> *"I'll take care of it. By the time I get back, I'll have worked something out."*
> *"To hell with Lutzi!"*

John finished reading and looked over at Roberta. She appeared to be in a trance. "Did you like that last one?" he asked.

Roberta snapped out of here reverie and when she spoke, her voice sounded hollow, far away. "Hmmm? Yes…er…it was lovely. Thank you, darling, you read beautifully."

She swung her legs out and sat on the edge of the bed. "Look John, I am going to head home. These damn cramps are going to keep me up half the night, and I'll likely keep you awake too."

"Really? Oh, that's too bad. Is there anything I can do, darling?"

"No, thanks. The walk home may take care of the cramps."

"Okay, I'll see you tomorrow."

"Probably not, because I have a pile of work to do on Angie's school project."

"Sweetheart, are you alright? Is there anything wrong?" John asked, concerned by her sudden change of mood.

"No, of course not. Why should anything be wrong? I'm just in a lot of pain with my legs."

32: The perfect crime

The next day, Cyril Caduggan had just returned from a meeting at Toronto City Hall when Roberta called him.

"Hey, boss. Any progress?"

"I did what you asked, Bobby. I spoke to our toxicologist. Had a long talk with her, in fact."

"What did she say?"

"Totally out of her league, apparently. She says the medical profession are way out of their depth when it comes to mycological toxicology. She says even the Poison Control Centre in Atlanta is hardly up to speed."

"Damn!"

"Hold on now, Bobby," Caduggan said. "She says the man you want to talk to is Albert Stultz. He's a professor of Pharmacology at the University of Wisconsin in Madison. Apparently he's one of the few experts outside of Europe. I've got his number, if you want it."

"Yes, please."

Caduggan read off the number, which Roberta scribbled on the edge of one of Bonnie's school books. "Bless you, boss. Thanks a million."

"You're supposed to be on leave, not working in cases. What's this all about?"

"A possible murder," she said, "and a very mysterious one, at that."

"Really? Well, be sure you don't go treading on the toes of local law enforcement."

"Don't worry. Local law enforcement won't go anywhere near this one."

"That sounds intriguing."

"I may tell you about it some time."

"Okay. When you coming back?"

"That's still up in the air. Maybe sooner than I originally expected."

~

Looking up the slope from the hayfields, Roberta could see that the old orchards, planted by Gillis family farmers many years before, were still laden with ripe fruit even though most of their leaves had vanished. Quite a lot of the fruit was shrivelled, starting to rot, or had been attacked by various insects, but she could still find enough for several pies.

A basket over her arm, Roberta wandered from tree to tree, ducking under the branches every now and then, searching out the best apples.

Behind the orchard, the house basked in sunlight, and a tiny spiral of wood smoke was rising from one chimney. Beyond the house, the wooded slopes rose steeply, the rich green of the softwoods being punctuated by bare branches or patches of rosy brown and burnt umber.

Above the buzzing of the last of the wasps and bees, the sound of the phone ringing came to her on the breeze. She dropped her basket and ran quickly to the house

On the window ledge in the kitchen the phone was ringing impatiently. Robert grabbed it and flung herself in the nearest chair.

"Hello."

"Sergeant Gillis?"

"Yes, this is she."

"This Albert Stultz in Madison."

The contrast between Roberta's surroundings and those of Professor Stultz could not have been more pronounced. His office, though spacious, was crammed with boxes, books and papers of every conceivable description. Some of the book piles mounted almost as high as the ceiling, blocking the light from the windows, while his desk was barely visible beneath dozens of files and notebooks. The professor was an overweight, balding man in his sixties with a large, grey moustache and gold-rimmed glasses. He wore a pin-striped suit and a bow tie stained with coffee.

"Ah, professor," Roberta said. "Thank you so much for returning my call. I am most grateful."

"Not at all. Thank you for your inquiry, Sergeant. It's quite an interesting business. A *very* interesting business. I've had a chance to consult the literature as well as talk to one or two colleagues."

"You have been busy," said Roberta. "I can't tell you how important this is to me."

"Is that so?"

"Yes, extremely important."

"Well, then, let me first deal with the matter of the species and varieties within the *Cortinariacae* order. You made specific mention of *speciosissimus* and *gentilis. Gentilis* is very common across North America and is highly poisonous. The other species is known in Europe and it may well be here, too, although we can't prove that. In the west they have something similar in *rainerensis*, but I have never heard of its occurrence east of the Rockies."

"That is very interesting indeed," said Roberta. "Please do go on."

"The actual species may not be especially important," continued Professor Stultz, "They can all kill because they all have what you referred to as *Orellanine*, a protoplasmic toxin, one of the cyclo-peptides. *Orellanine* is really two compounds, *Continarin A* and *Cortinarin B,* of which B is infinitely the more virulent. Are you still with me?"

"Yes I am still with you," Roberta assured him. "It is an awful lot to take in, but I think I've managed to make notes of the essential points."

"Good. Look, this is only significant in that *gentilis* has A, but *specisosissimus* has both A and B and therefore would be a much surer bet for your villain."

"Would there be significant differences in the symptoms, or are the effects similar?"

"Yes, similar. Destruction of the kidneys, which without immediate attention—in serious cases that would mean transplants—would probably mean death, and certainly I would think, in the case of *speciosissimus.*"

"And the kind of delay in the symptoms? Would they be similar also?"

"Again, similar, but depending upon the constitution and state of health of the individual and the amount consumed. There is hearsay evidence of cases where as many as nineteen days had elapsed between ingestion and symptoms. But your case—in the eight to ten day time frame—would be more usual."

"This *Cortinarin*—A or B—would it be detected in a post mortem?" Roberta inquired.

"No, not at all. Given the extraordinary length of time involved, the toxin would have become diluted and exited the system so that, by the time they started the examination, the culprit would have fled the scene, as it were. Even were that not the case, G.C.M.S, does not pick up biological toxins."

"G.C.M.S.?"

"Gas Chromatographic Mass Spectrophotomatry. That's what we call the screening process. In any event, the overwhelming majority of toxicologists have never heard of *Cortinarin* or wouldn't know what to look for. Do you happen to know if they kept any tissue? Because there might be a remote chance of picking up residual quantities of the toxin."

"No, professor, the police had no reason to be suspicious."

"What about the corpse itself? Where is that now?"

"The body has been cremated."

"Ah. Well," said Professor Stultz with great finality, "then we have the perfect crime."

"I'm afraid so," said Roberta. "I do want to thank

you most sincerely for all the time and trouble you have taken."

"I wish I could say it has been my pleasure, but under the circumstances I would have to rephrase that. I wish you well in your inquiries, Sergeant, but I fear that, short of a confession, they will be profitless. Goodbye."

33: May God forgive me

A glowing, pink sun had all but set behind the mountain, but its fleeting rays peeked over the crest and suffused the lakes and forests. Crows were showing off to some seagulls, and making a caco-phonous noise in reply to the latter's high-pitched wheeling.

It was cold, and both Roberta and John needed sweaters as they sat on the grass, looking out over the water. In the rapidly failing light, the vegetation on the far side of the lakes was still rosy, almost as if it were on fire, but their side was now in shadow.

Roberta had been quiet and withdrawn all evening and John, sensing something was afoot, watchfully puffed on his pipe. After a while he knocked it out on his shoe and stood up. "Okay, what's wrong, Bobby?"

"Why should anything be wrong?"

"You can't fool me. I can tell when something is troubling you."

He stood, looking at her waiting for an answer.

"Yes," said Roberta after a long pause, "you're right. Something is troubling me."

"Okay. What is it?"

"Something I have to tell you."

"That sounds ominous," said John warily, "What do you have to tell me?"

Roberta paused again, this time much longer. John stood motionless, waiting. "Well?"

"I'm going back to Toronto," she said simply.

"What? Going back? When?" John was clearly agitated.

"Soon. My month's leave is over."

"But didn't you say you could get an extension?"

"Yes, but I won't be asking for it."

There was another silence. Finally John said knowingly. "When you say you're going, you mean for good, don't you?"

"Yes. I do."

John swallowed, then carefully asked the question like a man who did not really want to know the answer. "Do you mind telling me why? Do you want to tell me why you want to throw away this marvellous thing we have together?"

Roberta did not answer.

"If you absolutely have to go back, for your work," John persisted, "I understand. Of course I do. I could come with you."

"No, you can't come with me," Roberta said very firmly. "That would never work."

"Why not, for God's sake?"

Roberta stood up and brushed the blades of grass from her pants. She turned away, looking across to Red Islands. The red on the trees beyond was fading. "I know you did it, John."

"You've lost me. Did what? What did I do?"

"I know you killed her."

"Killed who? What the hell are you talking about? You're talking complete nonsense!"

"You know who I mean."

John paused to collect his wits, then said. "Ahh! I see what you are driving at. I assume you mean that you think I killed poor Lutzi?"

"Of course I mean poor Lutzi!" Roberta's eyes were blazing as she turned to face him. "Who else would I mean? Do you know anyone else recently who has died under mysterious circumstances?"

"Let me get this straight, Bobby," said John, not looking at her. "Are you suggesting I murdered my wife? Is that what you are suggesting?"

"That's exactly what I am suggesting. Look me in the eye, John, and be honest with me. Did you or did you not murder Lutzi?"

Wearily, John walked up to her and put his face

close to her, his eyes searching her face. "Let me ask you a question. Do you love me?"

"Yes dammit, I do. I wish I didn't, but I do love you. May God forgive me for it."

"Well, you know I love you with all my heart and soul. I'd do anything for you."

"I know. That's just the point," she wailed, "That's just what I think you have done!"

"Love is supposed to be based on trust," said John, a little pompously. "How can you love me if you suspect me of murder?"

"Damn you, John Sedgemoor!" Roberta exploded. "Stop this dancing around! Why don't you just tell me? Be honest. For the love of God, tell me!"

"That's a no-win situation. If I say 'no' I can see you won't believe me, and if I say 'yes' I'm finished. How can I possibly win?"

"It's not about winning!"

"If we love each other," he said, tenderly taking her face in his hands, "and we do, the sensible thing would be to forget this conversation ever took place, and to carry on loving each other as before."

"It's no good. That won't work." Roberta was now sobbing. "I can't stop loving you, but I am a police officer. That's who I *am*. That's what I'm all about. Upholding the law, catching and punishing the criminals. It would always come between us. It would destroy us. Surely you can see that."

John nodded sadly, then let her go. As she dabbed her tears away with a handkerchief he paced along the cliff.

"All right. You're the smart detective," John demanded from a distance. "If I did it, as you say I did, *how* did I do it? I was three thousand miles away at the time."

"It was in the stew, John. That's why, when I asked you if there were any mushrooms, you said: 'one or two.' Why only one or two, John? Usually—if they were good mushrooms—you'd use half a pound of them...or more."

John stared at her, transfixed by her explanation. His face had fallen and showed the misery he was undergoing.

"I saw the book in your study," Roberta continued, "and the notes you made. It was either *Cortinarius gentilis or speciossissimus*—I don't know which. Either way, you knew that with her stupid prejudices Lutzi wouldn't go to a doctor when the symptoms started, and you also knew that she wouldn't die until you were safely out of the country. Quite an alibi—to be forty eight hundred kilometres away at the time of death. And just in case anyone was smart enough to analyze the deceased's tissue, you had her cremated. Very clever, John!"

John stared at her with new-found respect. "Even supposing, I say just *supposing* you're right, there are two inescapable conclusions. You know what they are, don't you?"

Roberta said nothing, staring at him defiantly.

"The first conclusion," said John, "is that because, as you have already suggested, I did it because of you, it makes you indirectly responsible."

"You bastard! How could you say such a diabolical thing?"

"Wait now...and the second conclusion is that, even if you're right, there is no way in the world you or anyone else could ever prove it."

They gazed at each other, both of them now in tears.

"I know," Roberta said very quietly.

"So, it will be an open file. One of your unsolved cases. I hope it doesn't tarnish your record."

Roberta snorted indignantly.

"What would you do, I wonder, if you could prove it?" asked John miserably.

"That I don't know," she said, giving him a long, sad, yearning look. "I just don't know."

She reached up and very gently kissed him. "Goodbye, my love," she said simply.

She picked up her flashlight, then turned on her heel and walked away down the hill. As the distance between them increased, Roberta sobbed uncontrollably.

Long after she was out of sight, John's lonely figure could still be seen on the clifftop, silhouetted against a rapidly-darkening grey sky that was streaked with gold and splashed with vermilion.

~

As Roberta drew level with the farm track to the MacDonald place, she could just make out Randy sitting on a fence, chewing on a piece of grass.

"Bobby!" He called out. "How she's goin'? Come and talk to me."

"Not now, Randy," Roberta said, hastily wiping away her tears." I have to get home."

Randy slid off the fence and came towards her. "Why, Bobby you've been crying?"

"It's nothing. I have to go."

"Aw, you've had a fight with your boyfriend."

"Go away, Randy!"

"You don't need to cry, Bobby. I'll take care of you. What you need is a little comforting."

"Randy!"

Randy slipped his arm around her. "I'll show you a much better time than that old fella up the road. Let's go up in them trees. You'd like that, wouldn't

you?"

"Randy, let me go!"

"Aw, don't be like that, Bobby," said Randy, trying to kiss her.

Roberta wriggled out of his grasp and violently thrust her flashlight into his groin. Randy howled with pain and dropped to the ground.

Roberta charged away down the hill.

Holding his injured parts, Randy struggled to his feet and ruefully watched her go, shaking his head in disbelief. "Holy Jesus, Bobby," he shouted after her, "you got one hell of a frigging temper on you. I likes that in a woman."

"Screw you!" Roberta yelled over her shoulder.

Breathless, she staggered into the driveway of the Gillis place and collapsed onto the front step, where she again dissolved into tears. When she had re-covered and recomposed herself she got up to go in-doors, but something caught her eye.

On the other side, under the trees on the bank, was a dark figure, standing, watching.

Overcome with absolute frustration and rage, she let out a blood-curdling scream and flew across the road. "You bastard!" she shrieked. "I'm going to get you, you pervert!"

As she approached, the figure darted away along the bank to escape but, missing its footing, fell into the ditch.

"Got you, you swine!" yelled Roberta.

She shone her flashlight on the figure, who was trying to claw its way up onto the shoulder of the road. There, caught in the beam like a deer trapped in headlights, was the watcher. It was Skit.

"Skit! It was you! It's always been you? Of course, the odour I detected on the bank that day was the cow shit you're always covered with! I should have known. What the hell have you been doing, you stupid creature? Are you out of your mind?"

Skit hobbled to his feet, whimpering and shaking with fear. "Don't be mad at me, 'Obby. I only 'anted to see you coz you're so beautiful. I only 'anted to see you."

"What? Oh, Skit. For God's sake, you prize idiot!"

"Don't be mad at me 'Obby. Please don't be mad at me. I loves you 'Obby." Skit whined, "Don't be mad at me."

"Skit, you've had me scared out of my wits. Following me, watching me. Can't you understand that is not acceptable behaviour? What on earth could you have been thinking of?"

"Don't be mad at me," Skit repeated. "I got a special present for you."

Skit rummaged around in his pockets and brought out a shiny object which Roberta instantly recognized.

"Dan's lighter! You stole Dan's lighter!"

"Don't be mad at me, 'Obby, I took it for you."

Skit thumbed the lighter, but it produced only sparks. Clearly it was out of fuel. "It used to make pretty fires, but it don't work no more," he said sadly, "Don't be mad at me coz it don't work no more."

She stared at him for a second, then it dawned on her. "The fires! Of course. Skit, what have you done? It was you who started all those fires. You desperate fool!"

"I was only playing with the shiny thing. Don't be mad at me."

Roberta gently took the lighter from him and, giving him her arm, helped him out of the ditch. Together, they lurched towards the house.

"Skit, you poor, pathetic creature. What are we ever going to do with you?"

She deposited Skit in a kitchen chair, and made him a cup of tea. Then she called the MacDonalds on the telephone.

Roused from sleep by the noise, Rod poked his head around the door. "What the hell is going on?" he demanded. "What's Skit doing here?"

"It is a terrible mess," Roberta said, "but I think I have it all under control. Go back to bed, Rod."

"Okay, Sis," Rod assented, then clumped back upstairs.

After a few minutes, a timid knock on the door announced the arrival of Lolly and Lavender, to whom Roberta related the entire sad, sorry story.

"The question is," she said, "what do we do with him now? Rightly, we should turn him over to law enforcement because, clearly, a number of serious crimes have been committed."

The MacDonald women looked at each other in alarm.

"If we do that, they'll put him in a mental institution where he'll be cooped up until he dies," said Lolly.

"We mustn't do that," Lavender pleaded. "Skit wouldn't last five minutes in a place like that."

"I'm a police officer. This puts me in an awkward position," Roberta said. "I've sworn to uphold the law."

The MacDonalds looked very agitated and Lolly began to cry.

"If we do as you want and brush this under the carpet," Roberta said sternly, "you must swear never to tell a living soul what you have learned here tonight."

"We will. We do," said Lavender and Lolly, their words tumbling over each other.

"And you must promise me faithfully you will keep

a very close eye on him. No wandering off, especially at nights."

"Okay," said Lolly, "You have our word. We promise."

"You hear that, Skit?" Lavender said. "You stay home now. Every night."

"Every night, yes," Skit said contritely. "I'm sorry 'Obby."

"I know that, Skit, and if you say it one more time, I'll brain you! Now go home, all of you."

Lolly and Lavender helped Skit to his feet. Then all three stumbled out to the yard and slowly made their way up the hill.

Pulling her coat around her, Roberta watched them go, thinking what a terrible day this had been, what a wretched, stinking, heart-breaking, absolute bitch of a day.

~

Most of the night had gone by this time, so Roberta did not bother to go bed, but made herself tea and whiled away the hours until she knew it was time for Rod to get up and go to work. She made him a coffee and carried it upstairs, being very quiet so as not to wake the children. She opened his door and crept in and switched on the bedside lamp.

Rod's bedroom was basically still the domain of his dead wife, Shirley. Even by the meagre light of the tiny lamp, everything in the room displayed a feminine touch. Rod had changed nothing and added nothing. In some ways, the room was his shrine to her memory.

Groggy from having been awakened, Rod propped himself up on one elbow to see Roberta sitting on the side of the bed, her eyes red-raw from crying. "What is it, Bobby?" he asked sleepily, "What's up?"

"I have to go, Roddie."

"Go? Where?"

"Back to Toronto. Back to my work."

"When?"

"As soon as possible."

"I hear what you're saying," said Rod rubbing his grizzled whiskers. "But do you really have to go so soon?"

"I can't stay here any longer. Not now. I'm so dreadfully unhappy, big brother."

"This must have something to do with Sedgemoor," said Rod, hitching himself up in the bed.

"Yes. And other stuff too."

"I think I understand."

"There's an awful lot I can't tell you—can't tell anybody—but it's all gone sour. If I stay, I'll be so miserable I won't be any use to myself or anyone else."

"Bonnie and Angie will miss you—especially Angie. So will I."

"I know that. I'll miss them, too. I've come to feel as if they are my own kids."

"When will you tell them?"

"Tomorrow night at supper. I want you to be there. I need you to back me up. For moral support. Will you do that?"

"Okay, Sis," said Rod. "You can count on me."

"How will you manage when I'm gone? Is there anyone you can get to help out?"

"We'll get by somehow. Maybe I'll ask Lavender. She's got a good heart and she likes kids."

"I hope the girls don't pick up her wanton ways." Roberta giggled through her tears.

"I thought I might do that," said Rod with a huge grin. "I could do with a little action."

They laughed heartily, then hugged.

"Now get out of here. I've got to get ready for work."

34: Moral dilemmas

The following day was fine and a little warmer, so Roberta took a farewell tour of all the nooks and crannies of the property with which she had re-acquainted herself with over the past month. She lingered in the orchard, enjoying again the mellow, ripe odour which hung in the air.

Then she wended her through the tall, uncut, yellow hayfields down to the shore of the Lakes. Across the bay, she watched a little boat sailing past MacLeod's Point and wondered who was in it and where it was going. It was likely, she thought, that John would also see the boat from his house.

Thoughts of John brought more pain, but also more guilt. She did not, could not, ever accept his accusation that she was indirectly responsible for Lutzi's death, but she was acutely aware that, through her silence, she was an accessory after the fact.

She knew that, without evidentiary proof, no law

enforcement agency anywhere would act on mere allegations, even from another police officer, and that in all likelihood they would think her deranged. If approached, John would no doubt say that he had ended the relationship and that she had invented a preposterous story out of revenge, a story authorities would be eager to believe.

Nothing whatever could be gained from her insisting that John be investigated, let alone charged, but that did not alter the fact that she had played fast and loose with the law. And, she told herself with anguish, she had done the same thing with Skit's situation. Although it might be argued that, in his case, she had tempered justice with mercy, it did not change the certainty that she had not upheld the law.

In this deeply troubled state, Roberta maundered about the grounds, kicking leaves and snapping branches. Glancing up the hill to her left, above the spruce trees, she could just see the roof of the old Ferguson house and she wondered, maybe even hoped, that John was feeling as wretched as she was.

She turned back up the hill and ambled up the path, past the weathered old barn and the overgrown garden, to the house. The children were not yet home, but she knew it would not be long before they came, and that soon after she would have to break the unsettling news to them.

Later, when they were all gathered around the table, Rod asked for their attention. "Kids, I have some bad news for you."

"What is it?" Bonnie and Brad demanded simultaneously.

"I'm afraid Aunty Bob has to leave us. She has to go back to her job."

A cacophony of cries and protests erupted, Angie breaking into tears. Roberta sat silently, staring at her plate.

"Look, I know it's rough on all of us," Rod continued, "but I've gone into this thoroughly with your Aunty Bob and I know it has to be this way. And I know that if your mother was still alive, she would agree with me."

Roberta reached out and squeezed his arm in appreciation.

"I'll miss you sooo much Aunty Bob" said Bonnie, touching her hand.

"Yes," wailed Angie. "You promised you would stay if I wanted you to, so please stay Aunty Bob. Pleeeze!"

"I know I've been a pain in the butt," said Brad, "But I'm going to miss you too."

As she went over to Brad and hugged him, Roberta began to sob. Angie ran around and clutched her.

"I'm so sorry, kids," Roberta said through her tears, "but it has to be this way. I must go."

Rod sat watching, like a man who had lost his way and had no idea if he would ever find it again.

35: One last goodbye

The next morning was even more emotional, first seeing Rod off the work, then putting the older children on the school bus, and finally—and most difficultly—parting with a sniffling Angie as Mrs. MacLeod collected her.

Roberta loaded up her car with suitcases and boxes, while on the front passenger seat she laid her road map, a box of candies, sunglasses and her purse. She took one last look around, climbed in and drove off. She had one more goodbye to make.

Dan was leaning against the rail of his deck when Roberta pulled into his yard. She got out, but made no motion to enter the cabin, staying by her vehicle.

"Same old story," said Dan. "You're not here five minutes before you're off again."

"That's life, Danny."

"Even lover boy couldn't talk you into staying."

"I don't want to go into that," said Roberta firmly.

"I don't know for sure why you're leaving, but I

think I can *guess* why."

"I have something for you," she said, passing him the lighter.

"My lighter! Where did you get it?"

"It's a long story, Danny. Let's just say I found it."

Roberta shifted her weight from one foot to the other and glanced at her watch.

"You've got lots of time," Dan said. "Did you see the master criminal before you left?

"No."

Embarrassed, Roberta walked round, climbed into her car, buckled her seat belt and wound down the window.

Dan leaned into the car. "Bobby, I can't promise I'll save myself for you indefinitely, but I don't plan on going anywhere, so if you ever need me, you know where to find me."

"Thanks, Danny. God bless."

"Goodbye, Sergeant," said Dan, turning away to hide a tear.

"Goodbye, Sergeant."

Dan watched the car back up, pull out of the yard then disappear down the hill through the mass of browning foliage. He picked up a few rocks off the ground, threw them to one side, glanced at the Lake, then he went into the cabin.

36: Nothing ever happens in the country

As always, the squad room was a scene of crowded chaos, and as noisy as bedlam. When Roberta came through the big, glass doors, there was instantaneous applause from her colleagues, accompanied by whoops, whistles, cheers and desk pounding.

Suddenly, she was surrounded by people, all talking at once. She felt whiskers rasp her cheek as Gordon gave her a brutal bear hug.

"Welcome back, Bobby!" he said with great warmth.

From the other end of the room, Cyril Caduggan came out of his office and strode towards her. He shook her hand and clapped her on the back. "Good to see you back here, Bobby. There were some of these goons who were betting we'd never see you again. Jenny here said she thought you would meet the love of your life and disappear into the sunset."

"No. nothing like that," said Roberta. "It's just that

I can't stay away from this place."

"I believe it" Caduggan said. "I always said that those quiet country places are all right for a short time to unwind, but you soon get bored with them. Nothing ever happens in a place like that."

"That's right," Roberta said. "Nothing ever happens in the country. Anyway, I'm back where I belong."

37: Gone

The sky was grey and inhospitable, with dark clouds twisting and turning this way and that. The hardwood trees were all bare, the branches reaching starkly into the bitter wind. Rotten, dark brown leaves tumbled across the road, disturbing the light scattering of snow which had fallen overnight. Some of the conifers still had a dusting of white on their needles.

Dan MacIssac's place appeared snug and hunkered down, piles of fire logs heaped against the windward side, while his boat, hauled up on land, was covered with a big, black tarpaulin. A single light burned in the old Gillis place, but smoke came out of one of the chimneys.

Further up the road, parked in a turn-off, Randy MacDonald's battered truck was shaking from more than the wind. Uncomfortably positioned inside, Randy and a young woman were locked in a lascivious embrace.

Looming up on the left was the old Ferguson place. The driveway was empty and the windows were boarded up. On the mailbox *Sedgemoor* was just visible. A large *FOR SALE* sign hammered into the front lawn stood like a melancholy sentinel.

The occupant had left and nobody knew where he had gone.

Jeremy Akerman

Highland Village Church

Acknowledgements

The author wishes to acknowledge invaluable assistance from Michele Raymond and Robert Bockstael (robertbockstael.com) in the preparation of this book.

The lyrics Roberta and others sing come from works in the public domain:

- The Water is Wide, assembled by Cecil Sharp from several folk tunes
- Skye Boat Song, by Sir Harold Boulton
- Good Morning to You, by Abbie Farwell Brown
- Down in the Valley, by Jimmie Tarlton
- Moonlight and Roses, by Jackie Braun
- (I'll Be Loving You) Always, by Irving Berlin
- It Had to Be You, by Isham Jones
- Bye, Bye, Blackbird, by Mort Dixon
- The Wheels on the Bus, by Verna Hills
- Silver Threads Among the Gold, by Eben E. Rexford

Jeremy Akerman

About the author

Jeremy Akerman is an adoptive Nova Scotian who has lived in the province since 1964. In that time he has been an archaeologist, a radio announcer, a politician, a senior civil servant, a newspaper editor and a film actor.

He is a painter of landscapes and portraits, a singer of Irish folk songs, a lover of wine, and a devotee of history, especially of the British Labour Party.

www.ingramcontent.com/pod-product-compliance
Lightning Source LLC
Chambersburg PA
CBHW070448200726
48293CB00007B/2142